Too Happy

A NOVEL BY

KATE KASTEN

ISLET PRESS · IOWA CITY

BY THE SAME AUTHOR

Better Days
The Deconversion of Kit Lamb
Ten Small Beds
Wildwood: Fairy Tales and Fables Re-imagined

Islet Press, Iowa City
www.katekasten.com
Copyright © 2017 Kate Kasten
ISBN: 978-0-9831959-7-9
Cover concept and lettering by Cheryl Jacobsen; photo by Barry Phipps
Typeset by Sara T. Sauers

To Caryl Lyons

Acknowledgments

I'M GRATEFUL TO Jen Adrian, Maureen Burke, Caryl Lyons, Anna Mary Mueller, and Denise Tiffany for their careful reading of the manuscript and their helpful comments and suggestions, and to Jean Frazer, Michele Gerot and Melissa Meisterheim for contributing their tshotchkes to the splendid cover design.

Thanks also to my new pals at Oaknoll—Madeline Bendorf, Mary Brandes, Shirley Dickinson, Judi Gust, Lucy Luxenburg and many others—for their support and kindness.

Best wishes, Lynne

Kate Karten

Prologue

$\mathcal{H}$OW OFTEN I have vowed not to get into this kind of trouble again. No more meddling. No more bending rules. The director of our program tactfully calls it "having a little too much empathy." I appreciate this. Kaye Bibber doesn't have a little too much empathy. She has just the right amount. She's fair. She's patient. She hasn't fired me. Yet.

But an administrator can be pushed only so far. I realize that, and I sympathize. I hate to be the cause of that angry flush on her neck whenever she's had to call me in. It's the only outward sign of what she's really feeling, that flush. She's a professional.

The first time I got myself into one of these pickles—years ago—it didn't raise even a spot of pink on her neck. She understood that I was just starting out in the field. I'd made a typical new teacher's mistake; i.e. having trouble "maintaining boundaries." Does that sound sexual? It wasn't. Far from it.

Here's what happened. I handed a student a tissue to staunch her brimming tears. Nothing at all of questionable judgment in that. But then I made the mistake of stepping around to the other side of my desk, murmuring sympathetic sounds and giving her shoulder a gentle pat. This had the effect of turning me, in the eyes of that homesick young woman (a stranger in a strange land), into a mother figure. And how could I extricate myself from the role without seeming, or in fact *being*, heartless, especially after she confesses, with lower lip trembling, that she has no friends here and can't tell her parents, after all their sacrifices, that she just wants to go back to her country. It was downhill from there. For two hours after all my colleagues had left the office for home and dinner, I heard her out and continued to utter soothing noises.

Thus was the precedent set for ever-escalating requests to "have meeting, just talk." Within days I was boxed into the role of mother, counselor, confidante and lifeline. Of course I shouldn't claim "I *was* boxed in"—the passive voice, as if to hide the agent—I boxed *myself* into the role. I admit it.

Kaye got wind of the situation—she always does—and brought me in for a chat. Was I aware that McBee University has counselors, foreign student advisors, a response team to knock on doors of depressed students? I was an English as a Second Language teacher, don't forget, not a suicide prevention expert or a degreed psychologist.

Yes, Kaye. You're so right. Thank you. I've learned my lesson.

Then the very next semester I had a perfectionistic student who collared me after almost every class and dominated my office hours with questions like, "Why that long sentence (i.e.: *The first people to cross the arctic land mass and eventually make their way down the North American continent into Central and South America were thought to have come originally from Asia during the period when the sea was covered by ice.*) hasn't commas?" How can a grammar teacher resist a question like that? (I wrote the sentence down and kept it for future reference.) The boy was so gratifyingly curious I really *didn't* mind spending the extra office hours with him. And midway through the semester when he brought me a gift to say thank you, offering it with both hands and that courteous little bow in accordance with Asian traditional respect for teachers, I simply couldn't bring myself to refuse it.

The gift was a set of fine hand-painted silk scarves, no doubt at a value far exceeding the three-dollar maximum mandated by the university. In the ESL Program, though, it has always been an unwritten rule that it's okay to defy this mandate by accepting the odd item that exceeds the price limit, in order not to insult students' cultural traditions. For example, a big box of loose-leaf mint tea fresh from a bazaar in Medina, Saudi Arabia, probably worth ten or fifteen dollars at our local organic food store, is openly shared among the staff by the teacher on whom it has been bestowed.

But this exquisite set of silk scarves could have gone for fifty, maybe a hundred dollars at an exclusive department store like Von Maur. The scarves certainly pushed the limits of our special exception to the no-expensive-gift rule. Nonetheless, I did accept them and even made a point of wearing the scarves to class several times to show the boy that his gift was appreciated. But I admit a small voice asked of me: Did you accept those scarves to spare that boy's feelings, or were they just too beautiful to resist?

Then the boy did a Jekyll and Hyde turn at the end of the semester. From a self-deprecating, grateful student who bowed respectfully upon entering and exiting my office, he became a belligerent, outraged young man upon learning that he had earned not a grade of A, as he expected, but an ignominious A *minus*. It was with great difficulty that I got him out of my office after showing him the scores that proved his work (despite his acknowledged diligence) had indeed earned an A-, and explaining that grades could not be negotiated. Too late I wondered if the boy meant the scarves to serve as a kind of insurance policy against the remote possibility of a grade lower than A.

He went straight to the Director. I had some bad moments waiting to hear Kaye's reaction. In the end, she backed me up without rebuke. I don't know if he said anything to her about the scarves. I don't think so. But when she came out of her office after the meeting, her neck was flushed well above her collar.

After this fiasco, I vowed not to be such a stickler about scores and grade equivalents but to reward effort. So the next semester, when an earnest and diligent student nonetheless earned a score of only 57% for the semester, I gave her a D- instead of failing her. Forgetting that no fruit on the class grapevine goes unplucked, I thought, What the heck, how can it hurt? The young woman's two slacker classmates, having missed half of their classes and failed the course, heard of their classmate's D-, stormed into Kaye's office and demanded to know why their scores of 58% and 59% respectively had earned them F's! They were being discriminated against! They would go to the Dean! They would go to the university lawyer. (Who knew international students back then would be litigious?)

Kaye had no choice but to raise the slackers' grades, much to the annoyance of the Registrar, who deeply deplores having to delve into the Byzantine student records system and take the many steps concomitant to changing a student's official grade. The color on Kaye's neck as she told me of this outcome crept all the way to her ears and was more mauve than red. She hates grade inflation. It jeopardizes the professionalism that got us our status as an excellent, fully accredited small program.

I went for several semesters without major incidents but over the years kept falling back into the soup. Kaye's flush began to spread up into her scalp, the crimson glow all the more conspicuous through her prematurely white hair. Not prematurely white because of me, I don't think. I'm pretty sure it's just genes.

So here I am twenty-four years later wondering, deep into the fall semester if Kaye will finally lose patience with me. Actually, worse than that, that she might be forced to fire me to save the University and the Program from being sued, giving the Dean of Liberal Arts and Sciences (the infamous Dean Beam) his excuse for getting the provost to outsource ESL instruction to his pet for-profit education program: *GET IN!* (More about this later.) The irony is that this semester started out as one of the most enjoyable of my career, despite the irksome presence of Chika Yamamoto.

·1·

THE ELEVEN INTERNATIONAL students of McBee University English as a Second Language Program Low Intermediate Grammar/Writing class—strangers to each other and sitting self-conscious and stiff-backed in their chairs—are waiting when I enter Room 420 South in the Slockett-Plum Building at nine a.m. on the first day of the 2009 Fall Semester. Just as an aside, I want to say how much I loathe Slockett-Plum. It's an immense glass-fronted rectangular box, embellished under the roofline with bizarre aluminum boomerangs meant to "resonate" with the nineteenth century Administration Building's Italianate brackets. S-P houses the School of Business and Finance as well as general classrooms. For me, it's haunted by the ghost of the mansard-roofed Victorian building it has recently replaced. In a single day's screeching, booming demolition, Old South Hall's high ceilings, echoing corridors, marble lintels and scent of chalk were obliterated.

Although, as I say, I loathe this over-air conditioned modern monstrosity, I have to admit that our fourth floor classroom offers, through its floor-to-ceiling plate glass windows, a stirring view of Zenith's spires and rooftops, and beyond these, the Eagle River, looking from above strangely like a gleaming metal cylinder where the water pours over the dam. Part of the vista is obscured by the top branches of the old Chancellor's Elm, Zenith's only survivor of the 1950's Dutch elm disease.

I stretch my arms toward the view and exclaim, "Oh, aren't we lucky!" and all but one of the students (predictably Chika Yamamoto) turn to appreciate it too. I haven't taught Chika before, but I've been privy to the despair she has produced in her past teachers. She has been held back in Low Intermediate level twice. This semester is her last chance to show she has at least a remote interest in studying and improving her grades. If she doesn't, Kaye will send her back to Japan. I hope I won't be the one who has to strike her out.

"Come on," I say, advancing toward the windows. Ten of the eleven students leave their chairs and tentatively step forward to look out at their American town. Just then, from a nest in the elm tree, two squirrels pop out on cue and chase each other from branch to branch at reckless speed as if assured of a net below.

One student declares, "In the Zenith is every places wild animal!" Another asserts that "In Beijing there have no wild animal except in zoo."

"The English word is 'squirrel.'" I say it, feeling a bit proud and authoritative. "S-Q-U-I-R-R-E-L."

The students laugh at their own attempts to pronounce the absurd *skw* consonant cluster and the tongue twisting *r* and *l* combination, and when they return to their luxurious upholstered swivel chairs, they rock gently, at ease and smiling. The ice is broken. Except, of course, with Chika.

❖ ❖ ❖

I take the roll: one Indonesian, one Salvadoran, one Tanzanian from the island of Zanzibar, one Kuwaiti, three Chinese, three Koreans, and two Japanese. Excellent. Thanks to McBee's diversity-focused international recruitment policy, there will be no large nationalistic cliques to break up. No need to constantly remind students to avoid lapsing into their own languages.

I introduce myself and give them permission to call me by my first name, Jane, instead of Ms. Frost, shocking the first time students, who are in the majority. In China, Korea or Japan, my title would be "Frost Teacher." The younger students will eventually get used to addressing me as Jane. Yumi Murata, a Japanese woman of sixty-four years, who sits erect and smiling with her books, pencil case, and binder piled neatly in front of her on the table, will never be able to manage it. Inevitably she will adopt "Teacher" or "Teacher Jane" as a compromise.

I had noticed Yumi Murata while proctoring the placement exams the week before. Yumi is the oldest student ever—just two years older than me—to enroll in the McBee English as a Second Language Program.

I should mention that I'm older than the other teachers here because I spent much of my earlier adulthood living communally and holding up hostile signs in front of certain corporate headquarters and military installations. Then at the age of thirty-five I made the momentous decision to pursue the needed credentials for a steady job in ESL complete with retirement benefits. So I feel a kinship with Yumi Murata, who daringly veered off her own track into a new life in a new land at age sixty-four.

As Yumi took the placement test, she hunched over the printed pages like a monastic illuminator, pinching her pencil tightly between thumb and fingers as she carefully filled in the circles on the answer form.

* * *

It's my custom on the first day to pair the students for a get-acquainted interview. After a little thought, I place Yumi with Masoud, a man of thirty or forty who is a refugee from the island of Zanzibar's earlier factional political violence. Unlike the other students, he is a permanent resident of the U.S.—the only one in the class who will stay after he finishes his education here.

The Salvadoran, Guillermo, announces, "Is okay for me *any* partners!" endearing him to me on the spot. I pair him with the solemn, buttoned-down Korean, Won, who reciprocates Guillermo's high-five just a beat late. Jiho, the other Korean male, I pair with the Chinese boy, Bing, who carries a lot of baby fat and looks barely eighteen. Bing is wearing a Chinese-made T-shirt printed with the English words:

Relax no more.
Activity.
Eat.

Probably meant only as decoration rather than philosophy.

Mi-young, a rather earnest-looking Korean woman of probably twenty-five, wearing a modest, belted shirt-dress and low heels, I pair with tall, slender, sullen nineteen-year-old Chika Yamamoto, dressed as usual in a mini skirt, over-the-knee mesh stockings and black high top tennis shoes. Her long black hair is streaked orange, and a look of contempt mars her otherwise rather pretty face. All last year she was famous for pouting relentlessly about her placement in Low Intermediate level, which, she asserted, was beneath her proficiency. No matter how gently Kaye Bibber explained to her that she had not placed at a higher level, and that there was much English she still needed to learn before being ready to matriculate into the University, Chika insisted that starting at Advanced level was the key to her early admission.

To punish her teachers and the program at large, Chika did no work, attended sporadically, and achieved F's in all her classes. I wonder if there is an expression in Japanese similar to the English "cutting off your nose to spite your face." Chika has earned her third semester in Low Intermediate level. Lucky me.

Among the remaining students is the pathologically shy young

Chinese, Zheng Zhijuan, aka "Fiesta," back for a third semester of harrowing public scrutiny. Customarily, the Chinese give their children names with meanings to live up to: Harmony, Wisdom, Diligence. Fiesta's Chinese name, Zhijuan, means Precious. But after having it repeatedly misunderstood and mangled by English speakers, she adopted "Fiesta," which, though strange and hardly apt, given her shrinking personality, is at least pronounceable.

Fiesta has progressed through Beginning level, High Beginning, and now to Low Intermediate—a monumental achievement for the virtually mute young woman. I gesture for her to roll her chair over to the two Muslim women—an effusive Indonesian, Mariam, and a tall, self-confident Kuwaiti, Heba, whose hair is covered by an electric-blue silk *hijab*. "Welcome!" Mariam cries, capturing the shy Fiesta's hand and ignoring her shrinking shoulders.

I sit back and contemplate the alliances I've just created. The partners dive quickly into the get-acquainted questions on their handouts: *Where are you from? What is your area of study/work? What surprising/scary/funny thing happened on your trip from your country?* These stories of mishaps and misunderstandings always open them up and get them going.

"Lady say me, 'Here or to go?' I think, '*heerdahgo*? Is she speak *English*?!'"

"Eighteen hours I'm coming by plane, then five hour at Chicago because tornado weather. *Tornado*! I call my mother. She say, 'Come back to home! Is too dangerous.'"

"Man on plane ask where I travel. I tell him Iowa. He say to me, 'Iowa! Why you want to go there?' So I'm worried it's danger place."

Unconsciously hugging themselves against Slockett-Plum's energy-gobbling cooling system, they grope for the words to express their complex thoughts in "baby English," as they self-deprecatingly call it. But at least they're all in it together. The students laugh and nod and interrupt, and I can already see them in four months—snapping each other's pictures, tearfully embracing, promising to stay in touch forever. For a few minutes I listen to their candid confessions. Then I take out my small drawing pad and indulge in my secret method for associating so many new faces with names. I start with a quick sketch of Yumi Murata.

Yumi must be a little under five feet tall. The thick shoulder pads of her pullover sweater give her the blocky torso of a diminutive fullback. Large pale-framed trifocals dwarf a rather punched-in nose as if it had once been broken. With a recent permanent wave, even her hair is a bit too big for her body. She is just two years older than me, but the lines in her face suggest many more years of experience—much of it harsh.

Her partner, the refugee Masoud, is a lean and reedy man with very black deep-set eyes and thick wavy hair that makes his thin face seem even thinner. Both Masoud and Yumi, I surmise, have lived many lives in one. I long to draw them at leisure, not surreptitiously, but when Guillermo and Won raise their hands for help, I hastily tuck the drawing pad into my binder and rub the tell-tale pencil smudges from my fingers.

After half an hour, the interviews show no signs of abating except in the case of the sulking Chika and her unfortunate Korean partner. Chika has set Mi-young adrift after hurrying through the questions with a minimum of conversation and rolling herself back to her original place at the table, where she sits desultorily engaged in the inspection of her split ends, strand by strand. Uncertain, Mi-young looks to me for guidance.

"Finished already? So fast!" I take hold of the arm of Chika's chair and, more abruptly than I intend, roll it back. "While the others are finishing, why don't you tell Mi-young about some good places to relax on campus. She's new here. What about The Hive?" The Hive features a dance floor, dart tournaments, pool tables, karaoke, and, on the week-ends, ear-splitting bands. I've heard it is Chika's favorite hangout. She met her American boyfriend there.

"It's bar," is all Chika will say.

* * *

I end the interview activity and assign the students, for homework, to write a paragraph about their partners. Then we begin the grammar lesson with a review of simple present and present progressive verb forms and usage. On the board I write, *I am teaching*.

"What does this mean?" I ask. "*When* am I teaching?"

"Now," several reply in chorus.

"You're right. I am teaching now. It's in progress now." I write "present <u>progressive</u>" on the white board. Then I leave the board and stand close to the long conference table around which the students are rocking slightly in their swivel chairs. "So if 'I am teaching' means I'm teaching *now*, what does the simple present, '*I teach*' mean?"

"Also now," asserts Heba.

"Also now?" I give it that teacherly, corrective uptone. Consternation breaks out around the table. Some students squint. Others grimace. Chika's eyes are closed and she appears to be taking a nap.

After a pause, the little Japanese woman, Yumi, raises her hand a modest inch.

"Teacher Jane? I'm sorry," she says, making an apologetic bow. "So *I teach* means I teach *in general, every day* because I am teacher."

Lights go on. I teach *in general!* Ah! Nodding heads continue to bob for several seconds in the wake of this insight. Satisfaction reddens Yumi's pouchy cheeks. Chika opens her eyes, looks at Yumi, and gives a little snort. I glance sharply at her and then quickly at Yumi to see if she has taken offense, but Yumi is still smiling as if in a state of bliss.

·2·

*W*HEN I COME BACK from Slockett-Plum to the English as a Second Language office after this first class of the semester, I arrive to a scene of commotion. In the reception area, a new Japanese student, weeping delicately into her hands, is being guided to a chair by Doug Best, the spectacularly handsome receptionist/secretary/cultural assistant.

Seeing me, he apologizes. "I'm sorry, Jane, I forgot to put out the sign."

Usually, the heavily bolded sign: **MCBEE ENGLISH AS A SECOND LANGUAGE STUDENTS THIS WAY ➤➤** is placed in the foyer the first week of the semester, to divert late arrivals from accidentally turning in at the Geology office across the hall and being brutalized by Gretchen Pettit, the Geology Department's ragingly territorial and xenophobic secretary.

Just FYI, English as a Second Language Program's offices take up most of the one-story pre-suffrage era Addams Hall, with its vintage 1917 wide plank floors, 1930s radiators and 1980s window air conditioners. We share this building rather too snugly with two other departments. One is Geology (consisting of the notoriously lazy and arrogant Dr. Gus Tamerius, his all-suffering junior colleague Dr. Richard Bloss, who writes the papers while Tamerius takes first billing, and of course Gretchen Pettit). The other department is

Linguistics, comprising the bashful and cartoonishly awkward Dr. Byron Stang and his loyal secretary Ginger Summerwell.

So anyway, after a twenty-two hour trip from Tokyo, including two long delays and a lengthy luggage search by Homeland Security resulting in her allergy medicine being confiscated, the new Japanese student is traumatized further by Gretchen Pettit's threatening reception.

"Don't worry, don't worry," Doug says to the girl gently. He lowers his six-foot two frame onto one knee, a hand hovering near the girl's shoulder without making actual contact. One consoling pat and he might inadvertently violate a university sexual harassment rule. Instead, he hands her a tissue and glances around for another Japanese student to translate and soothe. He spots Chika Yamamoto, who has beaten me back to the office and is waiting to pounce on the Director as soon as she should arrive.

No! I almost call out. Not Chika!

Too late. Doug has already beckoned to Chika, who sits in a chair by the door, sulkily fingering her bleached split ends, and indifferent to the drama playing out in front of her. At Doug's appeal, she looks over at the new girl, mumbles something to her in Japanese, and returns attention to her hair. Whatever she has said is not consoling. The girl weeps afresh. Chika has apparently given her unique point of view, the Japanese equivalent of "McBee ESL Program sucks."

If Chika is hoping to prevail on Kaye Bibber, One Woman Bad Cop/Good Cop/Program Director, to promote her, she will be disappointed. Kaye has already allowed Chika to move up to Intermediate level in Communication Skills, and that is a gift, although I will admit that Chika is very capable of making her demands understood. Kaye will listen unmoved by Chika's self-defense: "Last semester I was *already* study those thing like past tense!" Such self-incriminating complaints carry no weight with Kaye. Accept the

Low Intermediate placement in Grammar, Reading and Writing or catch the next plane back to Japan, she will tell Chika matter-of-factly. Kaye benefited from assertiveness training in the '70s.

Chika heaves impatient sighs each time the door opens and Kaye fails to appear.

"Hello again, Chika," I greet her. Chika pretends not to hear and stretches her long legs out so I almost trip over them. Just then, Yumi enters, all glow and cheer, bows to me and greets Chika in Japanese. Chika mutters something in return—something, judging by her tone, bordering on rudeness—but Yumi has come to ask Doug Best for an immigration form and perhaps doesn't hear it. The cheer doesn't leave her face.

"I love here!" she exclaims to the office at large.

On her way out, she notices the weeping girl and stops to say a few words to her in Japanese. The girl nods, bows, and utters something in reply. Whatever Yumi has said seems to have reassured her. She wipes her eyes and sits up straight, with a brave, all-is-not-lost smile.

After Yumi leaves, I turn my attention to Doug Best. Doug answers to any of the students' renderings of his name depending on the speaker's linguistic background: "Excuse me, Doge, could you maybe to help me, please?" "Dog! Dog! I am lost my visa!" "Thank you, Dogu Bestu, I'm sorry bother you."

"Good morning, Jane," Doug greets me in the slightly cracking voice that always reminds me of old high school flames. "Have a good vacation?"

"Very nice. You?"

"We bought two puppies!" His pleasure at this announcement brightens those soulful brown eyes.

"Congratulations. What kind?"

"Clumber spaniels. We spent the whole vacation training them." With a flourish he gestures at the background image on his computer—two low-slung animals with immense feet, outsize heads, and the slobbery jowls and drooping red-rimmed lower lids of elderly basset hounds.

"Adorable," I say, faintly.

·3·

*A*T THREE O'CLOCK that afternoon, Donna Bittner, our brand new teacher, fresh out of graduate school, puts her head in at my office door and wails, "I'm soo sorry to be late for our meeting! I had to run an errand after class and then I couldn't find a parking place up here, so I parked down below on the street and I ran up the hill, but—Oh God! Was that, like, meter parking? Of course it was! I forgot to put money in—" She begins pawing through a large rhinestone-encrusted handbag which hangs from her plump, bare shoulder.

Her off-the-shoulder peasant blouse reveals a startling amount of cleavage, and my first thought is of the horror Donna's Muslim students must have experienced at the sight of it and how I myself, being Donna's official mentor, will have to broach this delicate subject. Donna also has on a great deal of bling—glitter embedded in the rims of her glasses, sequins on the strap of her open-toed sling backs, rhinestones on earrings and wristwatch. Staring in fascination, I have to say I kind of like the bling.

"Oh God, I'm such a scatterbrain today. I didn't bring any change!" She gazes pleadingly at me. "I'd be *soo* grateful if you could loan me a quarter? I'll feed the meter and run and get change and repay you the second I get back, I promise."

I take four quarters from my desk drawer. "Please don't worry about it."

"Thank you so much. That's so kind of you! I'll be right, right back. I'm so sorry." She clasps her hands prayerfully at heart level. "Do we still have time to meet?"

I have to blink at a shaft of sunlight reflecting off Donna's glittering wristwatch. "Yes, I can stay until five."

"Okay, I'm going. I'll be back in a minute, I promise."

"Don't run up that steep hill," I call after her. "Please, take your time."

After she twinkles out, my office mate, Molly Askew-Ohashi, and I conscientiously avoid any exchange of looks or remarks. In the respectful environment of McBee English as a Second Language Program, it would be considered petty to express doubts so soon, even nonverbally. If we worked elsewhere, we might have scooted our rolling office chairs together and had a lot to say about this new hire.

* * *

When Donna Bittner returns, half an hour later, sweat glistening on her forehead from the walk uphill, she is carrying a goopy cinnamon roll, wrapped in paper, and a thirty-two ounce plastic mug from Café Gulp, the town of Zenith's local competitor to Starbucks. I introduce Molly and make space on my desk for the repast while Donna digs out of her glittering handbag a notebook and pen. I ask what made Donna decide on a career in ESL.

She worked summers for an accountant at a Los Angeles credit company, she says. All her friends had asked why she was crunching numbers, she was such a *people* person. Then she took a vacation in the Yucatán and met a Mexican diver who traded scuba instruction for English lessons.

"I fell in love! ... With *teaching*!" —Donna winks—"and that's been my passion ever since."

"Well, good. I think you'll like it here. It's a very congenial environment."

"Awesome."

I take myself in hand. Is "awesome" any less precise than "cool?" And didn't I still say "cool" on occasion?

I remind Donna that the McBee ESL Program, a language school housed within the university, provides intensive English classes four hours a day, four and a half days a week to prepare its students to enter U.S. colleges and universities. The ESL instructors are highly collaborative and Donna, at any time, should feel free to ask questions of me, her official mentor, or of the other teachers, or the Director.

"Wow!" Donna drops her jaw and shakes her head at such an unparalleled extreme of kindness. "That is so great! I know that you're all so much more experienced than I am, and I'll probably make a lot of mistakes, so I'll really appreciate any help I can get."

"So," I begin, "since you're teaching two very different skills and levels, one hour of Intermediate Communication Skills in the morning and two hours of High Intermediate Reading-Writing in the afternoon—"

"It's only my first day, but it's great so far!" Donna unwinds part of the cinnamon roll and holds it out. I decline the offer. She takes dainty bites of it, after which she licks her fingers as thoroughly as a cat.

"In Communication Skills classes," I continue, "we usually like to teach some pronunciation in addition to—"

"Oh, clear pronunciation just seems to come natural to me, probably because I did a lot of theatre in high school. We had to project, like, to the back of the auditorium."

"Yes, your speech is nice and clear, but—"

"The rine in Spine foals minely on the pline," sings Donna, with a great deal of vibrato. "They cast me as Eliza Doolittle because I happen to be gifted at accents. I can't take *credit*." She shrugs modestly. "I was born imitating voices. I've been doing it since—" She suddenly breaks off. A cat-that-ate-the-canary look passes over her face. Perhaps she's been training herself not to boast and has just caught herself in the act.

"Well, that's a very useful skill, but in addition to modeling pronunciation, you'll want to—"

"I was thinking tomorrow I might have the Communication Skills class do theatre warm-ups," Donna rushes on, recovering herself, "to help the students loosen up? We used to do a drama exercise where one person was the "naysayer" and the other was the "yeasayer" and we'd go back and forth saying "yes" and "no" in different moods—like guilty or suspicious or happy—"

Molly's chair creaks, and I imagine my office mate's fascination at the way the discussion is going.

"Donna," I say firmly, "let's talk about the curricula for the two classes—what the students should be expected to achieve by the end of the semester. And let's take a look at your plans for the courses, shall we?"

"Well, actually—" Donna takes another dainty bite of the cinnamon roll, then slugs down several ounces of coffee. She frowns at the plastic mug. "This isn't that great, for how expensive it was."

"How about taking a look at your textbooks and your lesson plans for this first week," I persist.

"Oh," says Donna, "wouldn't it be better to play it by ear for a while though? I mean every group is so different, isn't it? You can't really—" Suddenly she leaps from her chair. "Oh my God! I almost forgot!" She takes out a dollar bill and hands it to me. "Thank you so much for the change! You saved my life!" She dimples as she says this. In fact, a dimple pierces each cheek every time her expression shifts even slightly. Though this is just an accident of physiognomy, I can't help it, I find dimples utterly charming.

It takes several more tries before I can get Donna to discuss a tentative syllabus, and somehow, before she leaves, I have handed over copies of my own syllabi from the semester when I taught her courses.

"That is so awesome! Thank you!" she says, and jumps up to leave, cheeks dimpling, accessories sparkling, and bosoms jiggling.

·4·

ON MY WALK HOME I mull over the so-called mentoring session. What special qualifications had Kaye seen in Donna to choose her for the position? I seem to remember her mentioning a sterling phone interview and excellent recommendations from a highly-respected graduate program in California. Well, Donna will probably be fine, I tell myself. She's just inexperienced and possibly out of her element here in Iowa. Being a Californian, she's probably going through a bit of culture shock. At least she left the office absorbed in the study of the Staff Handbook.

I turn my thoughts to the pouting Chika, who, having finally collared Kaye that afternoon for a fruitless talk, huffed out, snubbing me as usual. I feel a flash of annoyance. Will I have to put up with this behavior for a whole semester? Absolutely not. I'll find a fresh, novel way to get through to her. I will. And I'll put my foot down, allow no more petulance, no more rudeness. But ... I know myself. Severity is not my style. Somehow I have to find a creative way to engage her. Something to do with art, maybe. Chika likes to draw, I'm told. This will be my challenge: to get Chika out of Low Intermediate level and on her way up by the end of the semester. Then, too, maybe something of Yumi's enthusiasm will rub off on her. Yumi's delight in learning will surely be contagious.

❊ ❊ ❊

Turning onto Green Street, my one-block cul-de-sac, I survey the 1920s and '40s bungalows, the tidy flower beds framed by picket fences or shrubs, and consider my own beds, a bit overrun with coneflowers and liatris. My small white bungalow trimmed in green, its lace curtains pulled shut, looks like a white cat in the sun with its paws tucked in and eyes trustfully closed.

But as I gaze fondly toward my house, I see, along the edge of the front yard, two decimated beds of what had that morning been pansies in full bloom. The rabbit is sitting smack in the middle of the street, its paws complacently drawn under itself and its ears erect in the classic rabbit pose.

I step off the sidewalk and go straight for it.

The rabbit cranks up its haunches for imminent flight but doesn't budge until I'm near enough to raise a scent. Then it hops a few yards away before sitting boldly down again, twitching its nose. I resurrect the vocabulary that I expunge from my lexicon when expressing myself in the classroom. The sturdy cottontail blithely leaps away, zigzags around the house, and disappears into the back yard.

"I'm going to fence the lawn and get dogs!" I shriek after it.

My helpful, elderly neighbor opens his front door and peers out.

"Rabbit," I explain. He gives an understanding nod and goes back in.

The loss of the pansies rather bursts my bubble of contentment. All summer the pansies have been my streetwise pals with their bulldog mugs and jutting jaws that warn, "Don't mess with me. I'm a pansy!"

❖ ❖ ❖

Corelli's Concerto Grosso #7 in E major has the perfect rhythm to walk around the house brushing my teeth by as I get ready for work the next morning. I rinse my toothbrush, switch off the radio, and gather up my keys and shoulder bag.

From my porch I see half a dozen jet trails, pink in the morning light, fanned out from the four horizons and crisscrossed at the top of the sky. Lawns are as green in late August as they were in June. The man who mows my yard finished at dusk the day before, leaving the smell of fresh-cut grass. All along the street, thick maples, trimmed around power lines, reach into the sky like a row of plush green mittens. At the end of the block, the beagle with the voice of a rusty hinge dashes toward me and flings itself against the fence. With the rabbit in mind, I think, too bad they have to keep this dog penned up.

I turn the corner and cross to the other side of the street. The minor pedagogical failings that nagged me from the previous semester—giving a test that was too difficult, rushing through grammar points that needed more time—have all but faded from memory, their lessons learned. The larger lesson, though—to quit meddling or bending rules—is once more fresh in my mind, and today I feel confident that those past transgressions will not happen again. With a new semester, new students, new classroom, new books, the slate is rubbed clean.

At the next corner a driver pulls away from a stop sign and casts a smile in my direction. I smile in return as I cross to the shady side of College Street. Where but in Zenith, Iowa, are people so diligently polite that they smile from a moving car when they accidentally catch the eye of a total stranger? My Asian and South American and Arab students—all from teeming cities of the world—ask the same question every semester: "Why do 'strange' people smile each other?"

Sometimes you need outsiders to show you your own home.

❖ ❖ ❖

That morning Chika Yamamoto slouches outside the classroom door with her American boyfriend until the very last minute. Allen is a beak-nosed, bean-pole of a boy with spiked hair and an upper-lip ring. He is waiting for her in the hallway, and in her hurry to get to him, Chika pushes past her countrywoman, Yumi Murata, almost knocking the little woman down. Yumi doesn't appear affronted, only startled. She stares at Chika with a bemused expression.

This day, Yumi is warmly cocooned in an oversized fleece sweat suit, socks, and white leather walking shoes. The other Low Intermediate Grammar/Writing students, too, with the exception of Chika, who sports a miniskirt and goose-fleshed thighs, are sensibly layered against Slockett-Plum's arctic air conditioning. They are ready with their interview paragraphs, double-spaced and typed in 12-point font. Even Yumi's is typed, though I had expected to have to teach her the basics of word processing.

"It's okay, Teacher, my name prints in up corner right side?" Yumi asks, anxiously.

"Perfect," I assure her. On the first day, Yumi had modestly murmured something about being "too old for learn new things." Quite the contrary. In spring semester, she had begun at zero level English at a community college ESL Program in Des Moines. In just one semester she has been able to transfer to Low Intermediate at McBee University.

Only Chika has failed to do the assignment. She turns away from mouthing a silent message to her boyfriend through the window in the classroom door, and on noticing Yumi adding her paper to the pile at my elbow, she widens her eyes in faux innocence and exclaims with disingenuous surprise, "We are suppose to write something?"

"*Were* suppose*d* to," I reply.

"I don't know about it."

Yumi helpfully passes her a copy of the syllabus, on which she has highlighted the assignment in pink and emphasized it with arrows. Chika pushes it back after a cursory look. I notice Yumi's eyes narrow and her mouth tightens, but just as quickly her smile returns, as cheerful as ever.

"I didn't know," Chika pouts, for my benefit.

"Chika," I say quietly. "Please come in to see me after your classes this afternoon."

"Why?"

She knows perfectly well why.

"Just because." I briskly take out my calendar and write Chika's name in the three o'clock slot.

"My boyfriend waits for me after class."

"That's okay. He can wait a little longer." I shut my calendar and start the day's lesson.

* * *

Apart from Chika, the students are all I could hope for on only this second day of class.

Because shy Fiesta was partnered with them the day before, the two Muslim women commandeer her as soon as she enters the room. She is now one of their own. Heba, the Kuwaiti, is in her late twenties and the oldest of ten children, she has informed us. This may account for her somewhat imperious and maternal personality. She tucks in the tail of today's flaming orange and magenta head scarf and calls peremptorily, "Fiesta, you come. You sit with *us*!" and Mariam, the Indonesian, her long, shining black hair swinging across one shoulder, takes Fiesta's hand and pulls her to the empty chair between them. Fiesta blushes and ducks her head, but I have to believe it pleases her a little.

I begin the lesson.

"Let's review what we learned about present forms yesterday. It's nine a.m. in Zenith, Iowa. What do you think the people in your family are doing right now in your country? Jiho, what are they doing in Korea?"

"They sleep."

27

"Right *now*."

Jiho frowns and twirls one of his many pocket pens. His silent countryman, Won, nudges him and whispers the answer in his ear.

"They are sleep*ing*."

"Good. Anybody else?"

Won's and Fiesta's and Bing's relatives in Korea and China respectively are also asleep at 3 A.M. tomorrow.

"El Salvador is same time as here," says Guillermo. "My family still are eating breakfast. Probably *huevos picados con tortilla*. Mmm," he says with an exaggerated swipe of his tongue across his lips.

"My little brother plays—playing—*is* playing—video game in bedroom," Mariam volunteers. "Because in Indonesia now is 11:30 today night. My mother go to there. She is saying him, 'Agus, shut up! Is too much late for game!' Agus say, 'You make me lose! I almost win!' Mama take out thing from wall—what you call it?"

"Plug. She pulls the plug."

"—is pulling the plug, and Agus says rude thing I don't translate." I can see already that Mariam tends to sacrifice accuracy for self-expression.

In Kuwait, Heba's parents, grandparents, two cousins, one aunt, five sisters, and three brothers (minus a brother who is studying with her here at McBee), are sitting down to an early dinner at 8:30 pm.

In Tokyo, Chika's mother is arguing with Chika's grandmother at 1:30 A.M.

Masoud, the only one whose family is living with him in Iowa, says wistfully, "My wife she is probably singing to my little boy a song." One hand unconsciously cups the air at the height of his child's head.

Yumi hesitates for just a moment before declaring that her "pasta maybe is playing."

"Your pasta?" The word translates itself in my head a beat too late to take the question back. "Oh, your pastor is praying?"

28

Yumi nods. "Every day."

"Your pastor is in Japan?"

"Pasta is here. Zenith Open Door Church." There is a fervent brightening in Yumi's eyes.

By what route has Yumi, from a land of secularists and a few old generation Buddhists, found her way to a charismatic, evangelical church in Zenith, Iowa?

·5·

I ALMOST WISH Chika wouldn't show up for the three o'clock meeting. What appeal can I make that hasn't already been made repeatedly by Kaye and every teacher in the program?

Chika doesn't wait for me to begin. As soon as she plops down in my student chair, she crosses her arms over her chest and announces defiantly, "My boyfriend says study grammar not necessary. I don't need. Also, he never study it."

No doubt. Grammar doesn't seem to be taught in U.S. schools anymore. Before being trained as an ESL teacher, the only English grammar instruction I myself received, even back in the old days, consisted of diagramming sentences and memorizing the fifty-two prepositions and the helping verbs, which I can still recite, to the tune of "Flying Purple People Eater." What good that has done me, I can't say.

"Native speakers pick up grammar as children by imitating their parents," I explain to Chika, as if she is actually listening. "They don't always need to be taught directly. But *non*-native speakers need to learn how to put sentences together so people can understand them—"

"My boyfriend understand me."

Oh yes. The language of love. Chika is gazing toward my open door. The boyfriend, expressionless, stands just outside the reception area clutching the waistband of his pants, which hang dangerously low on his skinny hips. Doug Best is offering him a chair.

"Chika," I say abruptly, "what is your goal for learning English? Why are you here? You've said you want to get into the University and study business."

She shrugs. "I just want to stay America."

"But you know immigration requires you to be a full-time student to maintain your visa status, and you also know that if you don't make progress after three semesters, McBee ESL will not approve a renewal. You'll have to go home."

"It's too boring. I can't study boring thing. Every semester I study same thing."

"You've *seen* the same information, but you don't actually study and apply it."

"I apply it enough."

I'm only making her defensive. I try introducing a more personal tone to the dialogue.

"When I took Spanish and French and Chinese, I had to learn their grammars in order to use the languages."

Chika cocks her head at this and looks at me skeptically. "You speak Chinese?"

"No, no." I've caught myself in my own trap.

"How long you took Chinese?"

"Only three semesters—" Chika opens her mouth to speak. "—but at a very low level and only for two hours a week and it was some years ago—"

"What you can say in Chinese?"

For a moment my mind goes blank. "*Nĭ hăo*," I say, weakly.

Chika sniffs. "Everybody can say, '*Nĭ hăo*.' It like '*Sayonara*.'"

But Chika seems to lose interest and doesn't press her advantage. She looks at her watch. "I'm going to Outlet Mall now. There's sale."

She gets up and, without thanking me for my time, flounces out of my office. The boyfriend jumps up and follows her past Doug's counter.

I didn't even get to the part about classroom courtesy: *How would* you *feel if your partners treated you coldly and refused to work with you?* I can imagine Chika's dismissive response: "Better not to always have partner. I can work by my own."

❧ ❧ ❧

After Chika leaves, I see Donna Bittner in the hall, walking at a fast clip and revealing just as much of herself as she did yesterday. She is clutching her glittering purse, apparently on her way home and in a hurry. I guess this is not the time to bring up the subject of her cleavage.

"How are things going so far?" I inquire as she passes. "Any questions? Let's get together after you finish teaching tomorrow."

"Oh, thanks," she says over her shoulder. "So far everything is *great!*" She stops for a moment to flash me that dimpled grin. "I'm just *so* grateful to be working with such fantastic teachers. You've all had *so* many years of experience—" and she dashes off, surprisingly nimble on her four-inch heels.

A stiffening sensation creeps up my back. Despite those winsome dimples, Donna leaves me with a vision of the oily flattery of Eddie Haskell in the 1960's sitcom, "Leave it to Beaver." *Yes, Mrs. Cleaver. No, Mrs. Cleaver. You're looking very lovely today, Mrs. Cleaver.* Now, Jane, I chide myself, Who—in the first semester of teaching—isn't over-eager and insecure?

Still, I can't shirk my duty. I will have to waylay Donna after class tomorrow. I can't let another day go by without confronting—no, not confronting—*consulting* with her in my office. Molly will be in class, and we'll have the office to ourselves. We'll sit down together and I'll help Donna see her revealing fashion choices from the students' point of view as strangers far out of their comfort zone. That will be a good way to put it, if a little trite. *Far out of their comfort zone*. I think it's a Donna-like expression.

* * *

Upon reaching my front yard that afternoon, I see that the rabbit has returned to finish off the pansy leaves and stems, eating them right down to the ground. Last June, I knelt in the dirt, rolled the pansies gently out of their containers, and set them in the holes I had prepared at some expense to my lower back. Where there had been only dead brown stubble from the winter salting of the sidewalk and crab grass reaching out its nasty tentacles, a throng of purple and orange and yellow and white and blue faces nodded at me in the breeze.

Now I scan the yard for the marauder, feeling genuinely murderous. The rabbit, however, is nowhere in sight. Too bad that the vigilant beagle down the street has to be kept behind a fence. Have I said that already? That's how murderous I feel.

That evening I sit at my kitchen table reading through my students' interviews with each other. Predictably, more than half of the students, on clear directives from their tuition-paying parents, who brook no back talk, are expected to enter a U.S. university as pre-business majors regardless of their particular aptitudes. Bing, just out of high school, aspires to sell luxury cars in his father's import business in China. Won is to enter the vague world of "financial," while Jiho and his parents see the good life in Statistics and Actuarial Science. Guillermo is thinking about either restaurant ownership or large-scale chicken farming in his native El Salvador.

Chika, too, is intended by her family to be a pre-business major when (if) she passes the international TOEFL exam (Test of English as a Foreign Language) and is admitted to the University.

Let me stray here a moment and explain the significance of

TOEFL. It's a standardized international test that students have to pass in order to get into U.S. colleges and universities. TOEFL is the gatekeeper, so to speak. There are cram schools all over the world that make oodles of money teaching students how to pass the test. The problem, of course, is that after memorizing the answers to thousands of example TOEFL questions and passing it, students haven't actually learned to use and understand English in the world of academia or any other world. It's very hard to convince students of this. Getting *in* is the main objective. After that, they assume everything will fall into place. It doesn't.

Fiesta, like the others, is doomed to study business, to what end, I can't imagine, given her excessive timidity. "Business," especially in the booming Chinese economy, is synonymous with success, prosperity, and security.

Mi-young wants to start as an executive assistant in some large Korean company and work her way up. I wonder if these students have an inkling of what it will be like to sit through years of marketing, accounting, statistics, management, finance and economics courses, taught by TAs using mind-numbing Power Point presentations. But perhaps they do have an inkling and think the MBA well worth the pain.

I get up and pour a glass of merlot before turning to the rest of the papers.

Heba, I discover, is already a practicing ophthalmologist in Kuwait and plans to become an eye surgeon, specializing in cataract surgery. Mariam wants to become fluent enough in English to get translating jobs that will allow her to travel the world outside of Indonesia. Will she ever get enough control over her sentence structure to make this dream come true? Yumi hopes to follow in the footsteps of the missionary pastor who brought her to the U.S. and sponsors her English study. Masoud, originally from Zanzibar, is a permanent resident in the U.S. He is determined to get a college degree so he can obtain any job better than his work in quality control on a toothpaste tube conveyor belt in Des Moines.

What must these students feel, reduced to two- and three-word sentences to express their complex thoughts? Students with an ear for languages race past their classmates, skipping to the higher levels and then on to academia, but the Fall 2009 Low Intermediate Grammar/Writing class appears, so far, not to contain such prodigies.

Still, I think of the Taiwanese movie director, Ang Lee, who would be solidly planted in Low Intermediate if he had to take our placement test today. Yet he directed *Sense and Sensibility*, the best film version of a Jane Austen novel ever made. Or I think of my German-born grandfather who retained an accent his whole life as dense as a block of Emmenthaler, but wrote a two hundred fifty page memoir in English without a single grammar or vocabulary error. So, you never know. Not counting Chika, Low Intermediate has enthusiasm in abundance. And that will take them a long way.

The three Muslim students—Mariam, Heba, and Masoud—have been fasting for Ramadan since before the semester began, and Yumi's paragraph about Masoud notes this fact with admiration. "After sun comes up Masoud does not eat food or drinking water. If sun goes down, Muslim eat and drink again. Every day they do like this for three weeks. What does it mean? They like to know the bad feeling so they understand more how does poor person feel who every day cannot eat or drink. It is very good thing like LOVE YOUR NEIGHBOR. Exception is children and sick and old people. And pregnant woman. It's okay they can eat and drink."

·6·

"MARIAM IS DANCER. She must show us," commands Heba on Wednesday morning when the class has assembled.

"No, no," Mariam demurs. "I need right music, special clothes, hair special way. Traditional dance have many things."

"Maybe you show just little part?" suggests Mi-young.

Guillermo starts the chant: "Mar-i-am! Mar-i-am! Mar-i-am!"

Mariam heaves an unconvincing sigh, kicks off her sandals and comes to stand barefoot in front of the whiteboard.

"This is *Tari Belibis*. Dance of … in English … wild water bird?"

"Duck?" suggests Yumi.

"Yes! Dance of Wild Duck."

For several minutes we watch entranced as Mariam, without music, bends and rises at the hip, moving her head and limbs in slow motion and extending her fingers and toes backward in graceful arcs as if every part of her were not firmly connected to neck, shoulders, elbows or ankles, but lifted by invisible wings. Each sequence of the ancient dance conveys what to me seems a precise syntax, so different from the often rambling incoherence of Mariam's English.

At the end of the silent performance, there is an explosion of applause while Mariam pads back to her chair and slides her feet into her sandals.

She shrugs. "Better with music and special clothes."

Mariam and the others are becoming more specific to me now, names and faces and ambitions coming together.

I look at my watch. There are still forty minutes before the break.

"Okay," I say. "So you understand present progressive now? What is it for?"

"Action happens now."

"*Is* happening now. That's right. However … " I pause ominously. "I'm sorry to tell you there are exceptions."

Guillermo smacks himself in the head. These mind-bending exceptions! Won, sage-like, looks off into the middle distance. He is certain to have memorized these exceptions but will not volunteer unless asked.

I write on the blackboard: *(1) I think … (2) I am thinking …*

"'I think Mariam is an excellent dancer.' Can I say this?" I ask.

"No!" exclaims Mariam. "I am not excellent dancer. My sister is dancer in my family take lessons at professional place can do every traditional dancing every kinds modern—"

"Okay, but what about the sentence? Is the grammar okay: 'I think Mariam is an excellent dancer'?"

They all agree, the grammar is okay.

"What does "think" mean here?"

"Opinion?"

"You believe."

"Your idea."

"Good. So how about *this*?" I lean my chin on my hand and stare into space for several seconds, frown and scratch my head. "What am I doing?"

"You are thinking!"

"So I can say, 'I am think*ing* about …'?"

"Toilet break!" This from Guillermo. The others laugh.

Masoud nudges him. "Don't think. Go!"

"I wait," Guillermo replies stoically.

"So imagine if I say, 'I'm thinking Mariam is an excellent dancer.' Does it sound right?"

"Should be I *think* because means 'I believe,'" asserts Masoud.

"Very good. So 'I'm thinking' sounds a little strange there, doesn't it? How about, 'Oh my darling—'" I clasp my hands to my heart. "'—I am loving you!'"

No it's wrong, they agree. Love is a feeling, not an action.

What are some things they love or hate, I ask.

"I love Bugatti. I hate learn verbs."

"I love my wife and my little Ali."

"I love bed, hate alarm clock."

"Good. Who can think of a strange-sounding example if you use "thinking" wrong?" Eyes narrow or gaze upward as brains are searched.

No one, it seems can think of an example. I realize that I myself am hard put to come up with another one beyond "I am loving you" and furthermore wonder at the wisdom of eliciting *wrong* examples.

Suddenly, without a word, Yumi pushes her trifocals firmly against the very slight bridge of her broad, punched-in nose, puts her books and binder aside, and stands up. With an imaginary set of chopsticks and an imaginary bowl held under her chin, she shovels imaginary food rapidly into her mouth, pats her stomach and closes her eyes contentedly.

"I am thinking mash potato is good taste," she says.

Mariam shrieks with delight. Even Fiesta laughs.

"It's wrong grammar. Should be '*think*," Yumi declares. She puts down the imaginary mashed potatoes and pantomimes a plate held at arm's length. With her other hand she picks something from the plate with the tips of her imaginary chopsticks, holds the item to her nostrils and screws up her nose. Then, glancing in both directions, she discreetly deposits the offending foodstuff on an imaginary napkin and throws it in the wastebasket. You can almost hear the thud.

"I am thinking cheese has bad taste," she says gravely. "Should be 'think.'" With her customary bows and apologies, she returns to her seat.

Guillermo and Bing and Jiho almost fall out of their chairs, and Heba laughs so hard she has to wipe tears from her eyes with the tail of her glorious *hijab*. Only Chika seems unimpressed.

"Thank you, Yumi," cries Mi-young. "Now I never use *–ing* verb wrong in my life!"

Who is this wonderful little woman?

There ensues the inevitable argument over cheese.

"Why Americans like cheese?"

"Cheese is not delicious," asserts Bing.

Guillermo, as a Central American, counts himself in with me. "With no cheese, *life* is not delicious."

I call break time, and Chika is the first out the door. The rest crowd around Mariam and try to imitate her flexible, backward-arching fingers.

At lunch, I think about Yumi Murata's cheese pantomime, such a surprise coming from an older woman from a country where students sit quietly, listen, take notes, and wouldn't dream of insulting their teachers by asking questions or offering comments. How strange that my best and worst students are both Japanese—one old, one young. But what of it? Am I trying to make some generalization about age, or about the Japanese? One always tries to put people in categories.

·7·

*O*PPORTUNITY TO TALK to Donna about her décolletage slips out of my hands once again. She is nowhere to be found before or after her class. The problem is growing urgent. Earlier in the day, Dr. Stang, the painfully shy Linguistics professor, averted his eyes when he caught sight of Donna bending over the drinking fountain, and Gus Tamerius openly leered at her as she passed the Geology office. But it occurs to me that I could get in some kind of trouble if I speak to Donna about her dress—or paucity of it. I would do well to check with the Director first.

I can tell Kaye is a bit irritable, just returning to the office after a morning meeting with Dean Beam, notorious for summarily merging and micromanaging departments. He has been hinting at the possibility of outsourcing the ESL classes to *GET IN!* (Gateway English Testing Instruction), the infamous purveyor of TOEFL cram schools that teach ESL students how to pass TOEFL without actually being able to function in English. *GET IN!* instructors are given eight weeks' training. The ESL teachers at McBee all have master's degrees. *GET IN!* doesn't employ marketing strategists for nothing; that *GET IN!* logo is irresistible, its forward driving italics suggesting an easy sprint through university portals. A *GET IN!* representative has come to McBee to drum up business recently, and Dean Beam has never met an outside contractor he didn't like. "Expedite" is his favorite buzz word.

40

✳ ✳ ✳

I follow Kaye into her office and shut the door.

"Kaye, I'm concerned about Donna Bittner's wardrobe, considering there are four devout Muslims in her classes. Even apart from the Muslims, it's a little over the top, excuse the pun."

Kaye sighs. "I noticed. Without a dress code, though, it's tricky." She smiles appealingly at me. "You're so good at broaching delicate subjects, Jane. Would you consider employing your famous tact?"

I agree to do it, but despite the compliment, I almost wish Kaye had forbidden me to say anything. Then I get a fleeting glimpse of Donna hurrying away from the copy machine in a low-cut spandex blouse that gapes between the rhinestone buttons, revealing a red brassiere. I know we will have to have the chat that afternoon.

✳ ✳ ✳

"Donna," I begin, "I wanted to discuss something with you—"

"Me too!" Donna interrupts. "Please, please, please could I change my classroom? It's like so old-fashioned!" Donna is teaching in the basement of the old Main Library. "How am I supposed to teach with just a dumb overhead projector? I can't play DVDs or go on YouTube. It even has a *chalk*board. It's like *prehistoric*!" A chalkboard. Whoa. *There's* a hardship. "I'm absolutely flabbergasted!" Donna exclaims.

There's a moment during which I mentally enjoy the unexpected use of the word "flabbergasted," a word my grandmother might have uttered. I feel a little affectionate toward my new colleague because of it, and anyway, it's hard to be annoyed with someone who dimples and frowns simultaneously.

"Well," I say, "I'll talk to Doug about finding you another room."

"That would be awesome!"

"But before you go, I need to talk with you—"

Donna glances at the large face on her rhinestone-encrusted watch.

"Oh my God I'm so late!"

She's out the door before she has even sat down. Once again, the cleavage discussion is put on hold.

❊ ❊ ❊

As I consider how best to approach Donna at the next opportunity, old questions from the Age of Aquarius rise to my mind: Does one person have the right to tell another how to dress? Why should women's torsos require covering up when men's don't?

On the other hand, there's the matter of cultural courtesy. The Muslims of both sexes in Donna's classes must, especially in each other's company, be finding the display of Donna's virtually exposed bosom extremely embarrassing. It isn't as if they had the option to look away. Donna's breasts, at students' eye level and framed by the blackboard, are situated at the focal point of the class. Then, too, there are the inevitable instances when Donna must walk about the room and lean in close to offer assistance. There can be no doubt that I have to speak to her.

How will she react? I recall my own disbelief when Mrs. Zwart, the Lincoln High School girls' Vice Principal, called me in to inform me that my hair was too big. *Too big*?! In 1963 girls would stand three deep at the restroom mirrors, wielding their rat-tailed combs and hair spray, teasing and sculpting their hair into gigantic poufs like football helmets. My own thin, straight hair needed a great deal more upkeep than others' but was certainly no bigger. It hadn't occurred to me that Mrs. Zwart may have been calling in *all* the girls who ratted their hair. In any case, no one stopped doing it, including me. What had I felt, upon being called in? Strangely, not humiliated, but indignant and defiant. Just what Donna would feel. *Absolutely flabbergasted.*

I must admit that while I deplore Donna's conspicuous cleavage, I rather enjoy her bravura in displaying it in such a sparkling setting.

Twinkling hopefully in my own closet for the last twenty years is a silver-sequined mantle, which I treasure too much to give away but am too cowardly to wear.

✳ ✳ ✳

The next morning finds Donna in a drastically minimalist state of dress again, it being a sultry August day. Taking a strengthening breath, I stop her on our way out to our respective classroom buildings to suggest a meeting that afternoon "just to check in about a few things." She'd *love* to, declares Donna, it would be *great* to get my valuable input, but she has to race off to a dental appointment right after class. Tomorrow maybe?

On the sidewalk, we pass one of Donna's Saudi students striding purposefully toward the ESL office.

"Aren't you going the wrong way?" Donna calls out gaily, shaking a finger at her. "Don't be late for class." To which the student ducks her head and keeps going. Donna says, in an undertone, "I just don't get that."

"Get what?"

"Why—if they're going to wear that scarf thing—they also wear Adidas? It looks weird, like they're trying to be something they're not. They should be one thing or the other."

Where to begin? But just as I open my mouth, our paths fork and Donna hurries off to her class.

✳ ✳ ✳

Though Donna somehow stymies my mentoring efforts at every turn, my Grammar/Writing class more than compensates me for my growing frustration. By the end of the first week, Low Intermediate Grammar/Writing is already proving to be the most satisfactory class I have ever taught, and I owe much of that to Yumi.

Before our first quiz, Yumi holds open her voluminous pencil case containing pens, pencils, pencil sharpeners, erasers, paper clips, highlighters and Post It notes as well as a mini stapler, white-out dispenser, scotch tape, and a tiny packet of Kleenex. Bing makes his typically fruitless search of his backpack for an eraser before plucking out a clean one proffered from her stash. Students often forget to return what they've borrowed from Yumi, yet her magic box is never depleted.

She is ready with offers of hot green tea from her thermos, extra paper cups, medicinals from her first aid kit: Chinese herbal flu preventatives, Korean headache pills, a chart of Shiatsu massage pressure points. This is all in addition to carrying eight textbooks, mono- and bilingual dictionaries, and a separate binder for each of her four classes. She hauls her supplies in a wheeled backpack almost as tall as herself, which she pulls up and down the hill to campus every day like The Little Engine That Could.

·8·

ON SATURDAY, I spend much of the day gardening. I wonder if winter pansies have arrived at the garden stores yet. I could protect the flowers from the rabbit by surrounding them with chicken wire, but that would completely spoil the effect. There is always cayenne pepper. It gives me a moment of shameful pleasure to think of the rabbit frantically rubbing with its paw at the burning sensation on its tongue. But even if I bought cayenne pepper, no sooner would I sprinkle it on those pugnacious little flower faces than rain would come and wash it away while the rabbit waited patiently in the shrubbery. No, I will have to resign myself to life without pansies. With this thought I spend a gratifying two hours ripping great clumps of creeping Charlie from my backyard beds.

Sunday I rejoice at having an entire uninterrupted day for drawing. When I throw open my curtains at 6:30 A.M., a thin shelf of pale pink clouds is suspended over the horizon, sunlight streaming underneath. After a quick breakfast, I set my drawing pad and pastel pencils on the back patio table and look around for inspiration. My neighbor's snowy white cat is picking its way through the emerald-green grass. At intervals the cat stops to shake dew from its paws. I pick up a pencil, but the movement sends the cat scurrying out of sight.

A morning glory vine bearing sky-blue blossoms as big as dessert plates has crept several yards through the grass overnight as if, having made a daring escape from the neighbor's trellis, it is trying not to call attention to itself. Then, suddenly, there is the rabbit. I, and it, at the same time, have fastened our attention on the same object.

The rabbit, swiveling its ears back in my direction, takes a few tentative hops toward one of the blue flowers. I rise. The rabbit pauses. We hold our positions for some seconds as the animal's nose twitches provocatively and my fingers quietly close around the rock I use as a paper weight. The rabbit leaps at the morning glory vine (which I half expect to rise up in a coil and hiss) and takes a preliminary nibble out of the blue flower. I pull back my arm to aim. But then, before I've quite gotten a bead on the animal, the rabbit turns its back on the blossom with apparent disdain, hunkers down in the grass beside it, and half closes its eyes, the very image of Albrecht Dürer's *Young Hare*.

I set down my weapon. Slowly, I lower myself into the straight-backed chair and study the rabbit. Fine white hairs outline the shell pink insides of its erect ears. Sunlight passing through them illuminates a delicate lacework of red capillaries. Ivory coronas surround its half-closed eyes. Against the grizzled brown of its back and head, a soft patch of rust at the nape repeats itself in the forepaws and along the sides, where it fades into the white of the downy underbelly. I pick up a brown pencil and set to work.

I finish the portrait by sketching the long black whiskers that spring from above the rabbit's eyes and around its nose. The whiskers add something comical to the image, like a child's cowlick that won't stay down. The whiskers, the straight-up pivoting ears and outsized back feet and legs, like someone else's parts patched on—a cat's, a donkey's, a kangaroo's—steal some of the rabbit's dignity, making it look a little ridiculous in its adaptation to the real perils of its life.

Does it get tired of the struggle? Maybe at this moment it's saying to itself, Yes, I know I should keep my eyes open in case this one charges as she always does, but all I want is to sit quietly and enjoy the deceptively sweet scent of these blue flowers and the breeze rustling my fur. All I want is to be lulled to sleep right out here in the open under the sun in a world without predators.

The rabbit's eyelids do drop a bit lower, and I think it might actually fall asleep. But the harsh caw of a crow overhead jars it from its reverie. The rabbit opens its eyes and twitches its legs. It waits for a moment, as if trying to decide whether the crow is going to make an adversary of itself. Then, without particular urgency, even perhaps with resignation, it hops away. I feel sad for the rabbit.

Cottontail with Blue Morning Glory is the name I give the portrait.

That afternoon I drive to Garden World. The last flat of drooping pansies is half price, so I feel less guilty for indulging in such expensive rabbit food.

·9·

I T IS MONDAY MORNING of the second week of the semester. Jiho, whom Guillermo has dubbed Question Man, shoots his hand up first.

"What means 'bingo'?"

"It's gambling game," offers Masoud.

"No. Can't be," Jiho objects.

"It *can* be a gambling game," I say, "but what was the context—the situation—you heard it in?"

"Grill lady at dorm cafeteria said to guy in my line, 'I'm guess you want usual fry onion on hamburger?' and guy said, 'Bingo.' Bingo is kind of food?"

Chika tosses her hair out of her face. "Guy means, 'You got it.'"

Slang! Here is something Chika can contribute. She's learned a bunch of it from her boyfriend.

"*Got* it?" Jiho frowns, still puzzled.

"Good, Chika," I say, encouragingly. Chika turns the compliment aside with a glance away. I write on the board: *bingo = Yes, you're right, you know it, you understand.*

Guillermo laughs and punches Bing's chubby arm. "Now I call you 'Bingo.'" Bing looks rather pleased, probably because Guillermo has given him a nickname and because it means "correct," which he so seldom is.

48

Mi-young brings up a strange question she has been asked by a server at a restaurant: "Are you interested in dessert adal?"

"What kind of dessert is it?" Mi-young had asked the server. She has heard of cake, pie, ice cream, cookies, but never "adal." The server enumerated several kinds of desserts and pointed to each on the menu. Adal was not among them. Finally Mi-young decided that he meant "add all." He was asking if she wanted some of each kind—maybe a sampler. She said, "Yes, thank you." This seemed to confuse him, and at this point Mi-young gave up and blurted out, "No dessert, please. Just I have coffee."

How to explain the polite softening and inherent irrationality of a question like, "Are you interested in dessert at all?' Either you are interested in dessert or you aren't. How does "at all" come into it?

I write the sentence on the blackboard and explain it as a set expression.

Mi-young shakes her head in defeat. "How can I learn all English strange things?"

❈ ❈ ❈

After the break, the students hand in paragraphs about culture surprises, and the class moves on to tackle articles: *the*, *a*, and *an*.

"What is the difference in meaning between these two sentences?" I write them on the board: "I saw a rabbit in my garden" and "I saw the rabbit in my garden."

Everyone stares at the sentences. Bing as usual whispers the words quietly to himself. Won's rapidly twirling pen tells me he has the answer, but will never volunteer.

I force his hand. "Won?"

He lays down his pen and clears his throat. "First sentence means general rabbit. Second sentence means specific rabbit."

"Yes. And what do you mean by general and specific here?"

He goes silent again. As is often the case, he can provide a rule but doesn't understand it.

"Well, let's imagine if I came up to Won," I tell the class, "and I said, 'I saw a rabbit in my garden this morning.' I already have a picture in my mind of the rabbit that I saw. In my mind it is a big rabbit with black whiskers and reddish spots on its legs. It eats my flowers. But does Won have a picture in his mind of this particular rabbit?"

Several heads shake, no.

"You're right. Won has no picture of this rabbit because this is the first time he's heard about it. So in his mind it's just some general rabbit, any rabbit, an indefinite rabbit."

"Surprise rabbit," offers Bing.

"Well, yes, you could say that. So how about if the *next* day I say, 'Hey Won, the rabbit was in my garden again today, eating my flowers.' Why *the*?"

"You want to stress about a rabbit?" suggests Mi-young.

"It's rabbit you talked before," says Mariam.

"It's the rabbit we talked about before, yes. Who talked about it?"

"Won and you," says Heba.

"Exactly. So *the* rabbit is a rabbit we *both* know about already. We both know which rabbit we're talking about."

Jiho waves a hand. "You said '*the* rabbit is *a* rabbit we both know already.' Why you said *a* rabbit in *that* sentence? We already talked about the rabbit."

"Ah."

Jiho, the Question Man, like a hawk, always homes in on the tiny mouse of a detail or exception that you really don't want him to notice.

Masoud's head is drooping. It bobs up just short of crashing to his desk. Jiho and everyone else except Chika are wearing the '*Huh?*' squint. Chika has turned around in her seat to face the window in the door. Behind it, the American boyfriend, Allen (whom Chika, unable to manage the medial /l/, calls Aaron), is waiting faithfully.

"Um, let's wait with your question," I equivocate.

Yumi bobs her head several times respectfully and says, "So, Teacher Jane, I'm sorry, thank you. If you say, 'Won, a rabbit lives in my garden,' I think your sentence *tells* Won the specific rabbit. It's rabbit in your garden."

Round and round we go. I take a breath.

"That's true, but—."

Masoud's forehead hits the desk hard enough to thoroughly wake him up.

I look out at the puzzled faces. Chika is breathing conspicuous sighs of impatience.

I must look flustered because Yumi jumps in once more.

"So. I told to my pasta: 'I take *a* Grammar/Writing class. *The* class is so funny because *the* teacher is so good.'"

The fact that Yumi, like virtually all my students, past and present, fails to grasp the distinction between *fun* and *funny* in no way lessens her contribution or my relief.

✳ ✳ ✳

I read the students' free-writing "culture surprises" paragraphs at home, where I can take the time to be fascinated by them before getting down to the work of commenting on them.

Yumi's paragraph contends ambiguously that "most men in America will let a older woman get on the bus first unless they aren't gentle" and observes that "there are many men keep holding the door when women enter to the door. I guess America do Ladies first. In Japan few men do Ladys first."

Won notes that in Korea students always hand in compositions with both hands while bowing, whereas "in here, students can throw paper on teacher's desk."

Bing admits to having three problems since coming to McBee. "One problem is that I can't treat increasing pimples. I have another problem that I can't eat fish." (Presumably because the fish sticks served in the dorm cafeteria are unpalatable.) "Third problem is I don't like most of American students." (He is living in a dorm with three American suitemates who spend most of their time drinking, watching movies on Bing's 42-inch TV, playing video games and ignoring the foreigner in their midst.)

Mariam writes that "there are always almost all people smile at me when my eyes meet the other people's eyes. I guess they show they never harm me."

Fiesta remarks that "Many Americans like to expose to sunlight directly for tan. In my country tan does not mean healthy. It might mean you are hard worker in the field."

Jiho appreciates the good fortune enjoyed by young men in the U.S., who, even though their country is engaged in two wars, aren't subject to a military draft as all Korean men are. "Republic of Korea Army provides young men with extreme stress."

Masoud once imagined that "there is a lot of crowboys in the U.S.", but has learned that there are none in Iowa, and that most exist in "ancient American film" such as "*Lonely Ranger.*"

Mi-young reports an upsetting incident: "My roommate cried last night. I said, 'What's the matter?' She talk very fast. I can't say, 'Say slowly, please repeat, I can't understand,' but I hear 'something something something don't worry about me I'll be okay something something something,' so I said, 'Okay, take care.' And it's late, I read in bed."

In her paragraph, Fiesta mentions having been told before she left China that in the "reach countries of the world, there were tones of poor people," but in Zenith she has not seen many—"one or two, but not tones." Well, I think, there are plenty of cities where Fiesta could see tons of poor people in this rich country, and she might

TOO HAPPY

never realize that quite a few people sleep under the bridge over
Zenith's Eagle River dam.

Chika hasn't turned in the assignment. She says "America culture
don't surprise me." Fine, nothing surprises her. But she needs to
write about *something*. I don't want to give her a zero for failing to
do the assignment. What about ... Of course! Why didn't I think
of it before?

I send her an e-mail:

*Chika— If you want credit for today's writing assignment,
you'll need to hand in at least a page on a topic related to
American culture. What about American slang and idioms?
You know a lot about that subject. Can you choose 2 or 3
idioms that you like or find useful and write about what they
mean, why they interest you, what contexts you've used them
in, etc.? You can have until Wednesday to hand it in.*

Clever idea, Jane.

·10·

I N CLASS THE NEXT DAY, Mi-young reports an update on the crying roommate. "My roommate said 'sorry.' She said something strange the reason she cried. She said, 'Johndear let my father go.' I don't understand that situation, who is Johndear, so I didn't know how I should answer."

On the board I write, "John Deere let my father go."

"John Deere is a big company in Iowa, but the economy is very bad now, right?" Everyone nods. They are all well aware of the global economic downturn. "So the John Deere Company is letting workers go." I write in big letters: LET GO = FIRED = DISMISSED = LAID OFF.

"Ah." Mi-young sees the implications. "So maybe my roommate has to stop study."

"In China," Bing pipes up cheerfully, "we laying someone *on*. Because many new companies. Many jobs."

And let's hope that Chinese bubble doesn't burst. Almost a third of the students in English as a Second Language programs across the country are now Chinese. Without them, there will be a lot of "let go" ESL teachers.

❊ ❊ ❊

After class, Bing asks me the meaning of "cloless."

"Maybe you mean clueless?" I suggest. I write it down for him.

"Yes, I think so."

"It means 'not knowing,' 'not understanding.'"

Bing gazes at the word for some seconds.

I ask for the context he heard it in.

"Two my suitemates come to suite with friend. I hear one suite-mate say, 'Where the CC?' Friend say, 'What's the CC?' Suitemates said together, 'Clueless Chinaman.'"

I am speechless.

"They mean me," Bing adds, without apparent emotion, as if it really doesn't bother him, as if clueless is as benevolent a nickname as Guillermo's "Bingo."

"I think," I tell him, "your *suitemates* are the clueless ones."

"They don't know me."

I have a momentary vision of myself charging into Bing's suite with a sturdy yardstick, snapping it over the roommates' heads and laying waste to their computers as they sit at their video games.

"Bing," I say, mildly, "would you like different roommates?"

"It's possible?"

"Yes."

"Then I think I want."

I stalk straight back to the Director's office to pour out the story. If Kaye thinks I am too involved, "having a little too much empathy," so be it.

This time Kaye's neck goes red on behalf of justice. She provides her minivan, and I my hatchback, and Jiho, Guillermo and Won also rally around. By the end of the week, Bing's computer, laptop, flat screen 42-inch plasma TV, Blu ray DVD player, home theater sound system, Wii console with remotes, and seldom used Wii Fit have been moved out. I rather enjoy the shocked and disoriented expressions of the suitemates when they come back to find their suite being denuded of entertainment electronics.

Kaye has found an opening in the International Friendship

Dorm, in the suite of Ted, whose Chinese suitemate has decamped for home mid-semester after getting word that his girlfriend back in China is cooling on him. The first thing Ted says on greeting Bing (even before he has an idea of the electronic windfall that's about to descend on him) is *"Péngyŏu, nĭ hăo!"* (Friend, hello!)

✻ ✻ ✻

When Kaye and I return to the ESL Program offices, she says, "Got a minute?"

She gestures me into her own office and toward a chair. Uh oh.

"Have you had a chance to talk to Donna yet?"

I look down at my nails. "I've tried to bring it up, but somehow she keeps slipping out of the conversation before it gets started."

"Well, one of her Saudi students came in this morning to ask for a move to a different class. She says she feels too embarrassed by her teacher's 'showing her body.' If she can't have a different class, she wants to transfer to a *GET IN!* school." We both grimace. "The student has a friend who goes to the *GET IN!* in Iowa City, and she can do the whole program sitting at a computer." Dean Beam would pounce on that bit of information.

We give each other a long unhappy look. Kaye says, "I suppose I should be the one to talk to Donna."

"No, no. I said I'd do it. I'm her mentor." (It never hurts to demonstrate that I'm capable of actions that don't bring color to Kaye's neck.)

"I'm surprised she doesn't have a better sense of appropriate classroom dress. She had such glowing letters of recommendation."

We sit thinking for a moment and watch the dust motes float in the sunbeams streaming through Kaye's south facing windows. I take off my too-warm sweater. It gives me an idea.

✻ ✻ ✻

"It's *so* nice of you to trade classrooms with me!" exclaims Donna on Wednesday morning, a very warm day for early September. "That's just incredibly generous. Slockett-Plum classrooms are so cool!" (Literally, I'm thinking.) "Thank you!"

I've caught her in her cubicle this morning before classes, me to my new classroom in the Main Library basement, replete with prehistoric blackboards and chalk, Donna, in another hour, headed for fully loaded S-P 420 South.

"You need the technology more than I do," I say with just a trace of her own manipulative Eddie Haskell sitcom character in my voice. "I don't need it so much in a grammar and writing class." Pulling a sweater from my bag, I remark, "It's a little cool in S-P, though. You might need this sweater today." Even Lady Godiva would cover up if she had to teach in Slockett-Plum. "And that brings me to something I'd like to talk to you about." My heart flutters. These confrontations are never easy.

Donna picks up a book and hugs it to her chest. Her mouth and eyes assume a neutral expression. Guarded. As if she has taken a step back.

"Do we have time?" she says, and now she does back away. She looks at her glittering watch. "You have to teach in ten minutes." She's afraid of being chastised. I can sympathize, but it must be done.

"If we need more time, we can finish talking later." I put my own books down on Donna's desk.

"Okay." She compresses her lips in a poor attempt at a smile.

I lean against the desk. "You know, it's my personal opinion that we should all have the right to express ourselves however we like in the way we dress. I could never work at a corporation where I had to wear a power suit and heels every day."

Donna frowns, her chin raised and head turned a little to the side as if taking in the information through a good ear.

"And we certainly don't enforce any kind of dress code here in the ESL Program, but we do have to think about the effect our dress has on our students."

"What do you mean?" Donna's frown deepens. It's a frown not of resentment but of puzzlement.

"I know it's the fashion these days for young women to wear … low-cut, form-fitting blouses and—"

"Ohh!" Donna seems suddenly enlightened. I have the impression she is, strangely, relieved. She unclutches the book from her bosom. The guarded expression leaves her face. She looks down at herself. "Too much skin?" she asks.

"Well, yes. Mostly because our Muslim students—"

"No problem," she interrupts. She sets her book down, snatches up the sweater I've given her, and buttons it up to her neck. "I would never want to insult anybody's culture."

No umbrage. No defiance. Why has this been so easy?

❉ ❉ ❉

Chika actually hands in her make-up writing assignment. There it is on my desk without my even having had to ask for it. At last! I've hit on something that engages her. All right, Jane!

"Good work, Chika. I look forward to reading it," I say, warmly.

"I get credit?"

"Of course."

I don't expect the grammar to bowl me over, but at least she's made an effort, and now we can look at the grammar one-on-one with this personally meaningful material to work with.

At lunch I take out the paper, entitled "Slang Words," and begin to read:

These are pretty common slang words. For example
1.   Give me a brake. you say it if someones pissing you off.

2. Duh means someone said something everyone knows. Its like that's pretty dumb.

3. Catch you later means See you later. Insted of saying goodby, you might say catch you later esp. if your going to see the person later

The essay is a list of fifteen such items. By the fourth one in this vein it's obvious that Allen/Aaron doesn't write, spell or punctuate well, but he knows where his duty lies.

❊ ❊ ❊

"Chika, please come to my office at 3:00 today to talk about your paper," I tell her the next morning. She shows up at 4:30, just as I'm about to leave. I ask her to take a seat.

"I got credit on my paper?"

I hand it to her. At the top I've written "zero credit—plagiarized."

She snatches it up. "Zero?! Why there is zero credit?"

"Because you didn't write this paper."

"I write!" she protests.

"No, you didn't."

"I did write. You should believe me."

"I'd like to believe you, but this paper is not yours."

"You said 'of course' I get credit. You *said*!"

"Of course you *would* get credit if you had written it. But you didn't. Molly and I have both talked to your class about the importance of doing your own work, not plagiarizing. Remember those lessons?"

"How you know I didn't write?" she demands. "You don't know."

"Chika," I put a blank sheet of paper on the desk. "I will give you credit if you show me that you wrote this." She lowers her eyes to the paper and folds her arms across her chest. "I'll give you an idiom from the essay you turned in, and you write the meaning and the context." I hand her a pen. She doesn't take it up.

"I can't remember same things I write before."

"That's okay. It doesn't have to be exactly the same words."

"But before, I have time to think, so I could write better."

I push a dictionary and our grammar book toward her.

"You can check your grammar and vocabulary. You can take as much time as you want. Here's the slang expression: 'Catch you later.' I'll write it for you." I write it at the top of the page. "Take all the time you need to think."

Sulkily, Chika picks up the pen and holds it above the paper for some seconds. Then she writes, "Its mean I talk you again other time. Later." As an afterthought, she adds, "Or maybe you hurry, so I can't catch now."

She drops the pen on the paper and folds her arms again. I slide the original next to hers and point out the differences in syntax.

"It's the grammar, Chika. Your grammar and this person's grammar are very different."

She gets up abruptly, grabs her backpack and walks out, muttering, "I don't care. Grammar is stupid."

Congratulations, Jane. You really motivated her

·11·

ON THE TUESDAY after Labor Day, the specter of World War II rises to haunt the student body of McBee ESL Program. On that day, I ask Molly to take the second hour of Low- Intermediate Grammar/Writing for me so that, in my role as mentor, I can observe Donna Bittner's 10 A.M. Intermediate Communication Skills class.

I'm not so concerned about her Advanced Reading/Writing class. Since this would be her first semester, we selected a very teacher-friendly Reading/Writing textbook for her, complete with a teacher's guide containing chapter and unit tests. I figure at the very least Donna can just "teach the book" this time around. Her Communication Skills text, on the other hand, requires more coordination of listening and speaking tasks and more teacher-generated lessons, so that's the class I feel the need to monitor.

I've made myself inconspicuous in the back corner of her classroom and have just settled in to watch an ongoing pair activity when a shouting match breaks out between two partners who are reading each other's writing assignment. Soon other students are rising from their chairs to join the battle, lapsing into their own languages—Korean, Chinese, and Japanese. The four Saudis and their Latin American partners draw together in consternation.

At the front of the room, with her hands on her hips, Donna shouts above the din, "Stop it! Don't be rude! Stop yelling!" As I step forward to intervene, the one Korean and two Taiwanese grab up their books and jackets and stalk out of the room, leaving two of the three Japanese students silently staring ahead with grim, closed expressions. Chika, also in Donna's class, is looking around her as if she's not sure what happened. The remaining students turn, goggle-eyed to me.

"It's no big deal!" Donna is shouting. "Just keep working!" I reach the front of the room and suggest, sotto voce, that it would be better to take a break for the rest of the period. For a moment Donna purses her lips, and then, flashing a peppy smile, turns to the remaining students and announces brightly, "Never mind. We're going to stop work. Class is over for this morning."

After a bit of probing, I discover the cause of the commotion. Donna has assigned a writing topic to generate a discussion: *What are some ways your country was affected by World War II or any other war fought on your land?* She came up with this idea, she said, from Googling "interesting discussion questions." As if the question were not sufficiently foolhardy, she then partnered two Taiwanese and one Korean each with one of the Japanese. They were to read each other's papers and comment on them.

The Korean and Taiwanese have all written paragraphs, quite similar to each other, accusing Japan of war crimes, with particular emphasis on the kidnapping of tens of thousands of Korean and Chinese women, including girls as young as ten, as "comfort women" for the Japanese troops. There have been articles in the newspapers and online recently about the Japanese government's continued refusal to unambiguously apologize for these atrocities or offer compensation to the surviving victims, whose treatment at the hands of Japanese soldiers left them forever emotionally, physically and economically devastated.

✳ ✳ ✳

"How was I supposed to know about that?" Donna expostulates, standing with her hands on her hips in her flabbergasted pose. "Anyway, it happened, what, like *sixty years ago*?" I have brought her back to the office to discuss what to do about the classroom explosion. "They weren't even *born* yet!" I sit and gesture Donna to a chair. She plops into it. "And anyway, isn't it a *good* thing?" she says brightly, "talking about *real* life, *authentic* topics—not just How I Spent My Summer Vacation?"

I lean forward, laying an elbow on the desk in what I hope is a friendly, but firm, manner.

"Yes, Donna, they do need authentic tasks in English. You're definitely on the right track, but—"

"Mint?" She has taken a box of breath mints from her purse and offers me one.

"No thank you. —But the treatment of China and Korea during the Japanese occupation was brutal, and even the younger generations haven't forgotten."

She puts several mints in her mouth and sucks on them. She's embarrassed. I hate embarrassing anyone. Will she feel better if I confess some humiliating pedagogical gaffes of my own?

I give her what I hope is a collaborative smile. "Donna, whenever we offer authentic practice, we risk making some kind of cultural miscalculation. I remember the time I brought the McBee Health Food Co-op representative to speak to my students for a listening activity. The Japanese students were giving each other the eye and trying not to crack up."

"Why?"

"It turned out they were very familiar with the rice cakes this woman was handing out as samples of adult health food. Rice cakes in Japan were only fed to babies."

"Really?" Donna is incredulous. "Why would anyone feed diet food to babies?"

"I suppose," I say, carefully keeping the sarcasm out of my voice, "the Japanese wonder why parents in the U.S. feed their children Big Macs." Donna seems to consider this.

I explain that our students are far from their friends and family and that although we want to push them a little beyond their comfort level—as she suggests—we still want the classroom to be a safe place, where they can disagree about issues without attacking each other or feeling attacked.

"Well, you'd think they'd be *over* it by now!" she blusters. But her hands tremble slightly as she puts her breath mints away. "Is this going to, like, get me in trouble with Kaye?" she asks, not meeting my eye.

"These things happen, Donna. Kaye will understand. We all make mistakes."

She looks up at me doubtfully. "Yeah, but on a scale from one to ten, how bad is *this* mistake?"

"Oh, no worse than some of the things she's had to call me in for … when I was first starting out," I add untruthfully.

This gets her attention. "Really? What did *you* do wrong?"

"Oh, things like being too strict or too lenient with grading policy rules." Maybe it will comfort her if I confess a little more. "I know better now than to get myself in fixes like that …" Do I really? "But even when you teach for decades, you can still put your foot in it. Kaye has come close to losing patience with me many times."

"What exactly did you do?" Her face is alight with interest. "For example."

I tell her the saga of the Korean boy, the scarves and the A minus.

"Wow! He was, like, *bribing* you?"

"Well, maybe not. But it was foolish of me to accept them."

I hope I've reassured her and given her an object lesson at the same time. This is good mentoring, I think, never imagining what I've let myself in for.

❊ ❊ ❊

In a hastily called meeting of the permanent staff the next morning, it's revealed that none of the disgruntled students showed up for Intermediate level Reading—the class following Donna's. The teacher for Beginning Reading reports that her students also seemed subdued that afternoon, word having apparently spread across levels during the ten-minute interval between classes.

Low Intermediate Reading/Communication Skills, however—the students that Molly Askew-Ohashi and I share—seem to be taking it in stride. I feel a little smug. We have two Japanese, three Koreans, and two Chinese, yet everything is copacetic. From my students I overhear just two comments about the controversy: "What's big deal? I don't interest in old war stuff." (Chika to her boyfriend) and, in an undertone, "Japan government must say sorry to Korean, must give compensate to Korean women." (Japanese Yumi to her Korean classmate Mi-young).

·12·

TENSIONS ARE REDUCED across the Program when Guillermo, always the social director, organizes a soccer match pitting Beginning and Low Intermediate levels (Red) against High Intermediate and Advanced levels (Purple). The teams play on the open field behind the Administration Building.

A little cheering squad from the four levels sits on a grassy rise above the playing field. Yumi has glued purple and red paper pennants to sticks and handed them around and cut red and purple armbands from strips of cloth for the players to wear. I, with the other teachers minus Donna, join. Where is Donna? Nobody knows.

Bing brings his new roommate, Ted, to watch. Billiards is Bing's game, not soccer. His father installed a billiards table in their large apartment in Beijing for the purpose of entertaining foreign business associates, and Bing has taken full advantage of it to become a pool shark, which may have accounted for his failing to pass his university exams and getting shipped off to the United States to get his act together. I've seen him recently at the Student Center in the pool room, humbling the American boys (possibly some of his former suitemates?) and passing on pointers to Ted.

Heba drops by the soccer field for a moment on her way home to start work on the mission statement for her application to medical school. She calls out to her twenty-one-year old little brother Mohammad a stern reminder to come home directly after the match. He has gotten a C minus on a composition in Beginning Writing class and is in the doghouse.

Masoud lingers at the edge of the field, longing to play. He's supposed to drive back to Des Moines to help his wife with his little boy and then get some sleep before his shift starts. But at last he can't resist the temptation and runs exuberantly onto the field to join the match for the first half hour before wrenching himself away.

Chika doesn't deign to make an appearance.

Once the match begins, Silent Won, leader of the Red team, shouts directives in English—"Back! Back!" "He's open!" "Go! Now!" which Jiho the Question Man follows unquestioningly as the players race up and down the field.

None of the women of Low Intermediate level has had the opportunity to play soccer in high school, but Fiesta and Mariam, it turns out, are athletic, and join the Red team, having learned the game from male brothers and cousins in childhood. Fiesta kicks with the aggressiveness of one who has been confined to a chair all day, and Mariam dribbles the ball around and past the running feet with her dancer's grace.

How the release from study transforms them all! The players leap and hug and high five whenever the ball gets past a goalie and disappears into the bushes. The fine, erect young shoulders—usually drooping after four hours hunched over paper and books—the strong muscular legs and arms, flushed faces, keen eyes, reflexes that, with the pivot of a foot, can reverse a headlong rush. Oh, to have a body again that can hurl itself into action without inviting punishment. The students seem like towering gods. Still, I cringe, thinking of the frontal lobes inside, when the players butt the ball off their skulls. All that tentative English in there, will it get rattled out?

When the match ends, the players jog over to the sidelines to flop down flushed and sweating amongst their cheerers-on. The Red team has won, and for that moment, Low Intermediate Grammar/ Writing's greater fluidity on the field more than compensates them for their lesser fluency in English. I admire them all. Perhaps even love them.

·13·

"**W**HY IN AMERICA everything is 'great'?" asks Bing on Friday, his cheeks shining like red apples under the fluorescent lights. "'Great' should mean 'very big.'"

Mi-young agrees. "I tell American roommate, 'Dryer empty now. You can use.' She say, 'Great!'"

"Even small things is great!" exclaims Mariam.

"Share French fry—'Great.'"

"Cell phone ring—'Great.'"

Gazing off into space through the curtain of her orange-streaked bangs, Chika murmurs disdainfully, "'Great' is just *idiom*."

Already the students are getting used to the wackiness of American idioms: "What's up?" "You betcha" "Get it together."

"Answer to 'What's up?' is '*What's up?*'?" asks Bing incredulously.

For many of the questions there are no answers.

"Why we can say American flag but not Iowan flag?"

"It's just crazy English," I reply, throwing up my hands.

Yumi tentatively raises her hand. "Teacher Jane? So I'm sorry, thank you," she says, bowing several times. "So. I think it is not crazy English. I think it is *interesting* English."

Interesting English. Better by far.

❊ ❊ ❊

Across the table I spread a mélange of photographs I have cut from

69

almost two decades of *National Geographic*. I hold up a picture of a middle-aged woman snorkeling in Caribbean waters. "Who is this woman? What is her job?"

"Teach swimming?" volunteers Yumi.

I tap the picture thoughtfully. "Maybe. But let's say she's a food server at a restaurant. What does a food server usually do? Fiesta?"

Blushing furiously, Fiesta opens her mouth and tries several times to choke out an utterance. Finally, like a cat with a hairball, she hacks up, "Gives menu?"

"Yes, good!" I rein in an urge to over praise. "What else? Others?"

"She takes people orders."

"She brings dish."

"She put water in glass."

"Fills glasses with water. Right. And is she doing those things now?"

No.

"What *is* she doing now?"

"She's searching fishes."

"She is swimming."

"She is enjoying vacation."

On my instruction then, the students crowd around the table to choose photos of their own. And while they sit absorbed in writing paragraphs about imagined occupations and current activities of unknown people, I feel the familiar pang. What is it about students absorbed in a task? Jiho's unconscious twirling of his pen over his thumb and forefinger as he stares down at his paper, Guillermo's restless knee, Yumi's left hand caressing the side of her face, and Masoud shaking his head gently as if listening to a blues standard. Bing, like a little boy, his round cheek almost lying on the table so that he looks as if he is writing in his sleep. Chika squinting at unbidden ideas pushing past her resistance and discontent.

Students' unawareness of themselves in these moments makes me want to press them all to my heart and tell them how lovable I find them, how even their smallest endeavors are indeed "great." I take out my drawing pad and sketch Guillermo—his appealing overbite, the eyes a little too close together and the stiff black hair swept into a peak at the top as if he had gone to sleep with his head wet.

❖ ❖ ❖

After the break, when we switch to a review of comparatives and superlatives, Bing pronounces the Bugatti the "most best car than Audi Q7."

"The Bugatti is much better than the Audi," I correct. "Or, the Bugatti is the best car of all."

"Can't say 'most best'?"

"I'm afraid not. There can be only one 'best'."

"In your mind," Yumi tells Bing, kindly, "Bugatti is most best, but not in English."

It had come out on that first day of getting acquainted that Bing's parents, who import high-end luxury cars in China, have agreed to give him a Bugatti if he gets very high marks in all his English classes. A safe bet.

Suddenly Yumi stands up and pushes her glasses against the bridge of her nose. A wide, exuberant smile spreads across her worn face. She proclaims, "So. This is the happiest time of our life!" Bowing and apologizing to me, she sits down again. Chika smirks. Yumi notices the smirk, and I think I detect a little color flare up in the hollows of Yumi's cheeks. Does Yumi's unconditional kindness have its limits? If so Chika would be the one to push them. Suddenly I have a juvenile fantasy of giving Chika a mean little pinch.

The others in the class, however, have erupted in cheers at Yumi's declaration. Guillermo jumps up and reaches across Mi-young to shake Yumi's hand.

"Low Intermediate … is … the best … class," he asserts, eking

out the sentence word by word to do the sentiment and the superlative justice, "because it has the smartest Grammar Grandma in
whole McBee Program."

Perfect superlatives and almost every article correct!

I assign them to begin a short compare-contrast composition,
and as I walk behind their chairs, I notice that Yumi, the Grammar
Grandma, while working on her outline, is humming a little tune.
I bend closer. I recognize the tune. It's "Blessed Forgiveness."

·14·

BY MONDAY Donna Bittner's students are showing a grudging willingness to participate, if not in spirit, at least in body. I've dropped in on the last fifteen minutes of her Communication Skills class, leaving my own students to free write until the end of the hour.

While part of my mind takes note of the high-pitched, kindergarten teacher intonation with which Donna praises the students' droning responses to an interminable drill she has devised, the other part of my mind is busy figuring out how to repair the damage to Donna's credibility.

"If they're going to sit there and sulk like children, that's their choice," Donna says after the class. "I'm not their mother," she adds, with a shrug.

I suggest that Donna ease the tension and satisfy the need for authenticity by bringing presenters to class—one or two professors from different departments or people from the community—to give the students a taste of the listening comprehension they will need when they matriculate into the University.

Donna makes a face. Who would she get? She doesn't know anyone here.

"I do."

The Geology Department's all-suffering Assistant Professor Bloss comes immediately to mind along with his public lecture for non-geologists, "Peeling Back the Layers of Time." The topic is of general interest, his enunciation is clear, his pace moderate enough for non-native listeners to keep up. I offer to ask him.

Donna considers this, her eyes narrowed in thought. As I watch, a light seems to come on. She begins to nod like someone who has just gotten the point of an esoteric joke.

"That ... is ... an *awesome* idea," she exclaims. "You are brilliant."

To what, I wonder, do I owe this veneration?

* * *

I e-mail Dr. Bloss on Tuesday and get an out-of-office auto reply. Reluctantly, I ask Gretchen Pettit, the intimidating Geology secretary, who is having her lunch in our shared conference room.

"Bloss isn't in town," barks Gretchen.

Her chronic attitude of being put upon is well served by the gravel in her voice, which gives the impression she has been nursing an unappreciative dying relative for several nights without sleep.

"And he's booked up solid," she rasps, "for the next three weeks. *At least.*" She adds, "Tamerius might have time to do it," enjoying my discomfiture at the suggestion. The tenured Tamerius is her other boss—the one who leers, and leaves Bloss to do all his grant work for him.

At this moment, Ginger Summerwell pops out of the Linguistics office and volunteers Dr. Stang's service as a speaker.

"I know he'd love to, for *you*, Jane," she says. For years her life's ambition has been to nudge Byron Stang and me into each other's middle-aged arms. "Dr. Stang has a great presentation on dialects of Kakchikel that he gave at the Rotary Club last year."

"Oh, but—" I begin, but Ginger is already brandishing Stang's appointment calendar.

"He's got a meeting with the Dean on Thursday at 10:00, but I'm sure I could get that re-scheduled."

"I wouldn't dream of—"

"It's not an *urgent* meeting." Ginger's emphasis radiates optimism. "But shouldn't you ask Byron first?"

"Oh no. He leaves his scheduling to me. And he's very accommodating." She crosses out Dean Beam's name and writes in mine. "You might not know that about him," she adds slyly.

Professor Stang walks into the conference room just then, and, blinking rapidly and casting his gaze in every direction but ours, mumbles his customary shy, courtly greetings: "Good afternoon, Jane. Good afternoon, Ginger. Good afternoon, Gretchen."

I can think of no further excuses that wouldn't impugn Byron Stang's suitability for the task. Briefly, I outline what Donna's class requires, emphasizing the ways in which an audience of non-native speakers differs from other groups he might have spoken to; i.e. their tendency to develop brain fatigue and to tune out if the English input lasts too long or if the proportion of unknown to known vocabulary is too high. "Especially if they're unfamiliar with the topic," I hint. Gretchen smiles knowingly. She wraps up her lunch and heads for the door.

Stang's brow furrows as he fixes his gaze at the top of the filing cabinet just over my shoulder.

"If you're busy, Byron," I plead, "don't in any way feel obliged—"

"No," he murmurs. "I'd be happy to."

Ginger, who has retreated to her cubicle, probably to give us some "alone time," pops out, saying, "I told you!"

In the hallway, Gretchen emits her mirthless laugh, like the uptake of a saw.

✳ ✳ ✳

"Have you thought about putting together a pre-listening activity and follow-up quiz for Byron Stang's lecture?" I ask Donna, receiving in return a blank look. "You'll want to prepare the students for unfamiliar vocabulary and give them a bit of background to help them take the lecture in."

"Oh. Okay, sure. But how am I supposed to know what he's going to say?"

I take Donna back to Linguistics to see if Ginger might have a copy of Byron's Power Point presentation that Donna can preview. Ginger swiftly prints it off for her and hands her a reprint of an article from *The Zenith Press Citizen*: "McBee Prof Studies Mayan Lingo." In the photo, the gaunt and pallid Stang stoops in the low doorway of a cornstalk hut, surrounded by short, brightly dressed indigenous women flashing gap-toothed smiles.

"Excellent!" says Donna.

❖ ❖ ❖

I picture the diffident Professor Stang standing before Donna's silent, sullen group of uncomprehending belligerents, blinking and murmuring his way through his Power Point presentation, throwing out arcane linguistic terms to explain a subject none of the students would understand or be the least interested in if they could. Or— my heart sinks—he will inadvertently fan the students' smoldering historical hostilities with descriptions of the government-sponsored genocide suffered by his Kakchikel Indian informants.

·15·

ONCE AGAIN I PREVAIL on Molly to take the second hour of my class so I can observe Donna's. I feel a duty to be there a little early when Professor Stang arrives to install the visuals for his presentation. Byron blinks several times at the screen of the computer into which he has inserted his flash drive, positions and repositions an anomalous-looking shopping bag on the desk, and unfastens and refastens his watch.

I observe it all from the rear of the classroom as Donna, innocent of what I am about to let her in for, showers Byron with such obsequious expressions of gratitude that he backs into the document reader and bends its arm. The students by now have straggled in, in a general slump. I close my eyes and draw a long breath before taking up my self-imposed task of suffering for everyone concerned. *Please, no mention of genocide*, I plead silently.

Professor Stang takes a step forward, flutters his eyelids and clears his throat several times before commencing. "Good afternoon," he begins. The students, brought up in cultures where it is unthinkable to leave a teacher's greeting hanging in the air, reply in unison, "Good afternoon."

Professor Stang does not seem surprised. He takes another step nearer his audience.

"I'm going to talk about a very old culture and its very interesting language. I am a linguist." He writes the word on the board. "Does anyone know the meaning of this word?" Calmly, taking his time, he stands and scans his audience's faces for an answer. His tics have fallen away, his eyes have stopped wandering. When no one offers a guess, he parses it for them on the board. "Here's a trick to help you figure it out," he says. "Does this part, *ling*, look familiar?" he says. "No?" He writes *language* and draws an arrow between the two roots.

"They both come from a word meaning 'tongue.'" He puts out his tongue and taps it. Several students chuckle. "Which we associate with speaking. And what about *–ist?*"

Even his voice quality has lost its constriction. It has taken on a suave, soothing, even seductive resonance. I can almost imagine him in a nightclub, boyish and bony like Frank Sinatra in his younger days, crooning, "*Strangers in the night, exchanging glances …*"

I can't see the faces of Donna's students from where I'm sitting against the far wall, but their erect backs, inclined slightly forward, show they are already engaged.

Byron brings up a slide of a map of Guatemala side by side with a map of Iowa. "This country, Guatemala, is approximately the size of our state, but in Guatemala there are fifty-four separate languages and dialects spoken." The students busily scribble notes for the quiz I have made Donna promise them. His short emphatic sentences are perfectly paced for an audience of language learners. Of course. He's learned languages himself. He's spent years speaking to the non-English speakers in his research.

For the next forty-five minutes, Byron Stang holds the students spellbound with his description of Kakchikel syntax, semantics and phonetics, comparing it in certain of its aspects to the students' own languages, all of which he has some linguistic acquaintance with. By the end of the lecture, the students can count to ten in Kakchikel and produce a fair approximation of the glottal consonants *q'*, *t'*, and *tz'*. The students linger so long to ask questions that they hold up the next class and have to be shooed out.

* * *

After Byron's talk, I walk with Donna back to her cubicle to discuss a follow-up quiz. The first thing I notice, apart from the always surprising deficiency of books on her bookshelves, is, still sitting on her desk, *The Zenith Press Citizen* reprint about Stang's work and the copy of his Power Point presentation.

To my casual inquiry, Donna exclaims, "I'm such a ditz! I got so busy, I totally forgot to copy them and hand them out before the lecture."

There is more to it than just handing the materials out, I remind her. Prior to giving students readings, she should plan how she wants to use them in a lesson. Yes, Donna was sorry, it was her "bad," but in a way hadn't it kind of turned out for the best, seeing how entertaining Dr. Stang's lecture had been? Knowing ahead of time what he was going to talk about would have spoiled the surprise, wouldn't it?

"Donna," I say, "when they're entertained, they pay attention. That's good, of course."

"Yes!" She pumps her fist in the air as if Team Donna has just scored a point.

"But—" I hesitate to seem critical, but I *am* her mentor. "We also have to help them *use* the language, not just passively listen to it."

Together, since Donna was so entranced by the lecture she failed to take notes, we construct a five-question quiz. Delicately I veto her suggestion for the first question: Name four of the dialects that Guatemalans speak.

"What are some general questions that reflect the students' understanding of main ideas, like: Why do the Guatemalan people speak so many languages? Remember? Dr. Stang emphasized that point."

"Great question! What else?"

Later, upon reflection, I realize that we didn't put together the quiz. *I* put it together.

·16·

MI-YOUNG HAS BEEN stoically enduring headaches off and on for a week. Her problematic American roommate laughed at her for saying she was going to "eat" medicine.

"My roommate said to me, 'Why you say *eat* medicine? Should be *take* medicine.' She think 'eat' is strange. But I don't take medicine like take piano lesson, take picture, take nap." Mi-young puts an imaginary pill up to her lips. "I *eat!*"

Mi-young shakes her head mournfully and winces. The headache is still with her. She has approached the wall of too-much-English-for-one-week, and the insensitive roommate has shoved her against it. Mi-young digs a finger into her right eye socket and tries to look attentive.

During the break, when I return from the drinking fountain, I find Yumi standing behind Mi-young's chair, pressing her stubby fingers deep into the base of her classmate's neck. Mi-young's eyes are closed and she breathes a blissful sigh.

Guillermo exclaims, "Dr. Yumi! I have very bad headache, too. And neck ache. And also backache."

Yumi lifts a hand off Mi-young's neck to shake a finger at him. "You faking," she says, playfully. "You are bad boy."

"What would we do if we hadn't Yumi?" says Mi-young, in an almost successful use of a conditional sentence.

"Yes, what *would* we do if we *didn't have* Yumi?" I'm a grammar teacher. I can't resist correcting.

Yumi shakes her head and waves off Mi-young's compliment as if taking a pass on dessert. She never allows herself to be praised.

* * *

I've discovered that on Tuesdays and Thursdays Yumi studies the Bible with a little Pentecostal university group, comprising a Ghanaian graduate student, an undergraduate American boy, and the Bible study leader, a young American woman who wears pastel dresses with sleeves gathered in a pouf at the shoulders and a heavy silver cross on a chain around her neck.

Occupying a table in a far corner of the McBee Student Center cafeteria, the four bend over their Bibles after lunch. I can't hear the discussion above the lunch hour din, but note Yumi's deep concentration. Having finished her favorite meal of beets and mashed potatoes, Yumi tilts her head to the side and closes her eyes. In this still pose, she seems not so much a woman as a little stone garden figure, a squat, flat-nosed Buddha. It would hardly have surprised me to see moss growing on her shoulders and a gentle stream of water dripping from her permed, gray-streaked bangs.

When Yumi comes into class after these Bible lessons, she has a tendency to hum—hymns, usually—in a thin, trembly soprano. Her serenity suffuses the room like sunshine through mist. "Hey," Guillermo shouts, "Time to start! Grammar Grandma is come," and the class takes up its study of gerunds and infinitives, modal auxiliaries, or whatever the subject is for the day. Several times Yumi has announced cheerfully, "I love here!"

It's difficult for me to imagine kind, forgiving Yumi accepting an Old Testament god who visits pestilence, slavery and genocide on backsliders and infidels, including infants and children, and especially hard to imagine her going along with the New Testament god, who condemns unbelievers to eternal torture. I suppose Yumi's Bible teachers have steered her away from the gory parts. Yumi proclaimed to me her dedicated adherence to "Love Enemy," "Turn Other Cheek," "You Without Sin Throw First Stone," and "The Gordon Lure" (which, after the sorting out of her confused r's and l's, reveals itself as the instruction to *Do unto others as you would have them do unto you*). These messages of unconditional love appear to be the key to Yumi's near constant state of bliss.

One manifestation of this bliss is her frequent urge to capture her new friends' images on film, which annoys Chika no end. She looks ugly in photographs, she says, but Yumi, like a determined little border collie, insists on rounding everyone up before the beginning of class or before they can get away at the end, and herding them into group poses. Occasionally, she runs into the hall and collars Chika's lounging boyfriend to take the photo with her old-fashioned film camera so that she herself can pose with the others.

❖ ❖ ❖

It has become obvious that all of my cheerful Grammar/Writing students are appropriately placed at the Low Intermediate level. Masoud hands in homework crumpled, stained, and damp from the sweat of his labors. When quiz results come back, he emits dramatic groans, while the bewildered Guillermo quips, with considerable irony, "A-plus for me *again*?" Question Man Jiho immediately thrusts a hand in the air, while Won hastens to consult his talking digital dictionary, forgetting, in his eagerness, to turn down the volume on its startling voice and causing everyone to jump. Won, whose name sounds like "one" and whom Guillermo calls "The Silent One," confines his speaking to pair work, and then only reservedly. Not on account of shyness, it turns out, but as a matter of principle. He stays after class one day to explain to me that he doesn't believe in talking in school; in Korea it isn't polite. Furthermore, one shouldn't speak unless one has something sincere and original to say. Tactfully, he refrains from criticizing his countryman Jiho's propensity for popping up with questions at a moment's notice.

Chika barely glances at her tests before stuffing them in her backpack, while Mariam immediately snatches Heba's to compare scores. Their protégée, Fiesta, learns to slip hers very quickly into her notebook.

Yumi frequently claims to be too old to learn easily. It's true that her speech is halting, but there's nothing wrong with her memory, and she's a natural language learner. She arrives early to every class, hands in all assignments, and scores above ninety on tests.

Yumi is close in age to Chika's dictatorial grandmother. The grandmother—as Chika loudly and frequently complains to her boyfriend outside the classroom door—constantly presses her parents to summon her back to Japan and get her married before she becomes a "spoiled wedding cake." Her mother wants her to stay at McBee to get into the Business School and find an entrepreneurial husband. ("But I don't want marry," she declares to the boyfriend. "It's better single girl." I wonder if he's relieved to hear that.)

To Chika's extreme annoyance, her mother and grandmother call every other day, urging her to study and cautioning her to cook Japanese food and "not get fat like American." Her grandmother sends packages of healthy Japanese bean paste confections, which Chika passes on to her classmates, not from any generous impulse, but because she disdains foods from her country now, preferring the Big Macs and Taco Bell burritos that her boyfriend enjoys.

Apart from being Japanese, the one thing that Chika and Yumi have in common is their desire to stay in the U.S. Yumi is not ready to go back to her country. She is "too" happy here, she says. (I've explained to the class that "too" doesn't usually mean "very," and that it implies a negative: "This coffee is too hot to drink," but it's hard to break them of the "too" habit, though I suppose it's possible to be too happy, if it sets you up for disappointment.) Yumi has told us that on finishing her English classes she hopes to move to Springfield, Missouri, and study at the Bible college that her pastor graduated from.

The Muslims had been observing Ramadan during the first weeks of classes. Suffering from sun-up to sun-down fasting, they were hungry, thirsty, and tired all day long. In the first week, Yumi came to class bearing a large Styrofoam cup of whipped cream-topped latté from the Slockett-Plum coffee cart.

"If no coffee in the morning," she declared, lifting the cup to her lips, "my mind like traffic jam." Then she remembered her deprived Muslim classmates, who stared longingly at the twenty-ounce container of caffeine. "Sorry, sorry!" she said, and with no hesitation, capped the container and shoved it under her chair. "Now our minds in traffic jam together." Masoud, Mariam, and Heba gazed at her as if smitten. After that, no one brought food or drink of any kind to class, even breath mints, until Ramadan ended this last weekend. On Monday after the Eid celebration ending Ramadan, Yumi brought everyone Japanese snack packages printed in English with the description: "Chocolate coating Cake. You that sweet things make smile we love to see you smile with your people. So just taste this cake." Everyone did.

·17·

"How did the students do on the quizzes over Dr. Stang's talk?" I ask Donna. It's been a week since last Thursday's lecture.

"Oh wow! I almost forgot about the quizzes. I haven't had a chance to grade them yet."

How long does it take to score 5-question short answer tests, I'm thinking.

"It's probably a good idea to get them back while the information is still fresh in the students' minds."

She thrusts out her lower lip in a mock pout. "My bad. But, honestly, how could they forget that great lecture?"

"Still …"

"Don't worry. I was going to grade them today and give them back tomorrow."

I'm starting to feel like the parent of a teenager. How old is Donna? Twenty-three? Twenty-four? Am I supposed to be mentoring her, or nagging her?

* * *

I've promised myself to stop micromanaging and let Donna make her own mistakes, but when I run into her on my way to the office after our morning classes the next day, I can't resist asking her if she graded the quizzes. She smacks her forehead audibly.

"Oh my God, I graded them and forgot to give them back! I'm such a ditz!"

She rummages in her bag and pulls out the tests. Sure enough, she has graded them. I see a big red A on the top quiz. One of her students passes by on his way to lunch.

"Sangkyun!" Donna shouts, startling him by grabbing his arm. She thrusts the tests into his hands. "Would you do me a huge favor and hand these out to your classmates when you get to Reading class?"

I swiftly pluck the tests from Sangkyun's tentative grasp and send him on his way.

Donna frowns. "What?"

When she was in grad school, I'm wondering, did she sleep through the FERPA briefings?

"Donna, have you heard of the Federal Education Respect for Privacy Act? FERPA?"

"FERPA? Really? FERPA? It sounds like what you do after too many tequila shots."

Good one.

"Yes, I know. We all have our FERPA jokes. But if you *violate* FERPA, you can get yourself and your program in big trouble."

"How?"

I explain that we don't let students see each other's grades without their permission. Even their parents can't know their grade if the student is eighteen or older. "So when you give back tests, you need to hand them back individually and face down."

She takes the tests back from me with a little sniff of annoyance. "Well, okay," she says. "I wouldn't want the FERPA police on my case." And she clomps away on her platform heels.

* * *

It's close to the end of September, and I call all my students in for progress conferences. Yumi comes for her appointment on Thursday afternoon.

"Teacher Jane, this your children?" she asks, pointing to a 1950 photo of my parents, brother and sister, and myself as a three-year-old on my mother's lap, the whole family perched together at the top of a Lake Michigan sand dune.

"It's my family when I was a child." The old Kodachrome color intensifies the blue sky, my mother's bright red lipstick, our golden tans.

Yumi picks up the photo and tilts her head to peer at it through her trifocals. "It's you?" I nod. "You were so happy girl," she says, with a suggestion of wistfulness, or possibly envy, in her voice. "Your mother was happy, also, I think."

At this remark I feel obliged to qualify the happiness so evident in the picture. "My father had been away in the war a long time, and my parents were very glad to be together again." The happiness on their faces is emblematic, it occurs to me, of the safe, secure upbringing I was privileged to know.

Yumi sets the picture on the desk so abruptly it falls on its face. She sets it upright, apologizing. She says after a moment, "Your father was soldier."

It sounds like a revelation. A soldier. What does it mean to Yumi?

"In *Europe*," I hasten to add. "My favorite memory," I say, to change the subject, "was crossing Lake Michigan on the ferry boat every summer and feeding the seagulls. It was wonderful. Did you spend any time at the sea with your family?"

Yumi drops her eyes.

"I can't say," she replies.

It isn't the first time I have made this blunder with Yumi. Some days earlier, to get the students to practice the past habitual mode, I asked them to write anecdotes from their youth. "When I was a child," I said, by way of illustration, "I used to blah blah blah … or, My sister and I would blah blah blah …" The students always get a kick out of *blah blah blah*. But Yumi, wearing a troubled look, left her seat to confer with me privately.

"Teacher Jane, I'm sorry," she said in a low voice. "I can't write. I'm sorry."

"Can't think of anything to write about?" I asked, ready with suggestions.

She bowed several times. "So. I'm sorry. Thank you. Just I can say I was rough girl."

Rough, as in tomboy? Or did she mean she had a rough childhood? Molly, Yumi's Reading and Communication Skills teacher, had warned me that there were things Yumi didn't want to talk about. I've learned this much: Yumi is single, retired from many years' employment in a Tokyo factory where she worked a machine that sprayed lacquer on bento boxes for restaurants.

Now in my office, Yumi looks up at me with an open countenance again, just as abruptly as she had shut herself off.

"Jesus help me every day," she says. "Before Jesus, so I was very bad condition. But now everything is good." She attends Zenith's only Pentecostal church every Sunday. "Whole day, I go. Also I go other days. Pasta talk. I talk."

"That's very helpful for your English."

"Yes." Yumi nods. "First time, I understand *this* much." She makes a tiny gap between her thumb and forefinger, and then opens them to a space of about an inch. "Now I *this* much."

I hold out my hands and spread them wide. "Yumi, it's at least *this* much."

"Thank you. No. So I improve a little because good teachers. But I am still so bad. Thank you. Thank you. No."

We've gotten off the subject of God, but I can't control my curiosity. "How did you become a Christian?" I ask. Yumi's face seems to sag. There I go again, overstepping the bounds. "Don't tell me," I hasten to reassure her, "if it's too personal."

Yumi looks past me at the picture on my desk. "Whole my life was very bad time," she says in a subdued voice.

I calculate that she would have been an infant when the war ended. Her family must have endured hardships. Maybe her father had been killed as a soldier. Maybe they were at Hiroshima or Nagasaki and she had become orphaned.

But Yumi recovers her serenity. "So. But last year in autumn time I find lady who showed me God. She said come America, and God send me to here. Now I am too happy every day."

For a year, then, she has been in this state of grace.

"I don't ever alone now! In future time, maybe I can be pasta, too," she exclaims.

I have my reservations about Christian evangelicalism, yet I'm glad for Yumi that she's found solace, even at Zenith Open Door Church, where frenzied shouts of "Praise the Lord" can be heard on Sundays through the open door.

But it is definitely time to move to a less loaded subject before I get myself in too deep. "How can I help you to reach your goals in learning English?" I ask.

"Thank you. Thank you. Nothing. Nothing. I satisfy. Teaching is perfect. You give me already too much. Thank you."

I forbid myself from having favorites, but how can I resist Yumi? Despite her old-fashioned Japanese tendency to bow and apologize and disparage her own proficiency, she is proving to be the most outgoing and "proactive" learner in Low Intermediate Grammar/Writing. Her announcement, "This is the happiest time of our life," has cheered me along with everyone else.

·18·

IN CLASS TODAY, with Yumi's inspiring words ("I love here!") in everyone's ears, her partners have thrown themselves into the Snakepit game, hissing and forking their fingers extravagantly at each other for failing to append the final *–s* in such sentences as: "Every morning my mother eat pomegranate" (Mariam), "On weekend, my roommate boyfriend sleep in her room" (Mi-young).

Following a run of perfect sentences, Yumi (with a knowing glance at me) leaves off the rest of her *–s* endings (allowing her less accurate partners to save face, I realize). "So," she says. "My pasta *read* Bible three *time* every day." She dodges, laughing, when they poke forked fingers at her.

Then, an incident that seems so small, so commonplace, changes everything, though I'm not quite aware of it at the time.

❋ ❋ ❋

After the break, the students work on superlatives—*the best, the worst, the least, the most*, etc. They've devised crosswords with the names of important people in their lives. Yumi's example contains my name. Having spent considerable time at home with her dictionary and thesaurus, she has come up with a flattering set of superlatives about me and has written it on the board:

The **J**olliest
the f**A**irest
the most i**N**genious
the kind**E**st
Grammar/Writing teacher at McBee school!!!

From Chika's corner comes a provocative snort when Yumi reads this aloud. I haven't known Yumi to possess such a thing as hackles, but I can almost see hers rise at this snort, adding a good inch to her stature. I choose to ignore Chika's provocation.

The next day, Yumi presents me with a glossy, framed photograph of myself surrounded by my students and smiling broadly beside this monument of confidence in me—the jolliest, fairest, etc. teacher at McBee. She presents it to me as soon as Chika walks in the door, late, as usual.

Since that snort, an uncharacteristic and troubling stiffness has marked Yumi's interactions with Chika for the first time.

I'm starting to feel uneasy about it. Enough is enough, I decide. Something must be done about Chika. I'm not going to let anything, even the smallest iota of annoyance rob Yumi of the happiest time of her life. Clearly Chika isn't to be managed. But how, *how* can I shape her up when every other teacher has failed?

❊ ❊ ❊

On the weekend, I take myself to the University Museum of Art. My mind always opens up in art museums, even in this one where the permanent collection is as familiar as my own hand.

I wander into a room that houses large abstract origami sculptures created entirely from the intricate crimping and folding of single five-foot square sheets of homemade paper.

Which makes me remember a workshop I took several years before, "Drawn into Learning," where I was shown how to create a tiny eight-page comic book by making several folds and a single cut in an 8 ½ × 11 inch piece of paper. On each page the participants drew images reflecting what they had learned in the workshop.

Here at last is my idea! The margins of Chika's textbooks are covered with doodles and cartoons. That is the one thing she has no trouble concentrating on—drawing.

I plan the lesson carefully—first a review of how to use the past progressive verb form: *was/were+verb+ing.* Then examples off the internet of minimalist cartooning styles—stick figures, a cartoon consisting entirely of text inside thought balloons, one whose characters are all represented by single dots. These will impress upon the rest of the class that one doesn't have to know how to draw to make a comic book.

I make eleven templates on blank sheets of paper, showing the fold and cut lines. Then I make a model—my own comic book illustrating the past progressive. In panel one I draw myself as a stick figure with pageboy haircut and glasses on a string. The caption reads, *I was walking to work this morning ...* In the next panel a stick figure cat appears and stick figure me holds a hand out to it. *... when I stopped to pet a cat.* In the third panel I'm kneeling on the sidewalk next to the cat. *While I was petting the cat ...* and so on.

Not too fancy. Not too intimidating for non-artists. Really a clever idea—multi-intelligences, different learning styles, all that. Motivated to draw the comic book, Chika will naturally put some effort into the captions; i.e. the verb aspect. And not just Chika, but the whole class. Learning made fun. Really, I'm quite proud of myself.

Before heading for class on Monday, I show Molly the lesson plan and the little example comic book I've devised. She leafs through it, exclaiming over the pages as I try not to hover. "Cute!" "Funny!" and "You're such a good artist!" she says before handing it back. "I can't draw worth a darn."

This is not the reaction I intend. Chika might take to the idea, but will the others be daunted?

They are indeed. Heba folds her arms and looks stern. Perhaps drawing cartoons is beneath her dignity. Fiesta panics. "Draw picture?" she asks, as if I have asked her to strip naked. Guillermo jokes disparagingly, "I draw person like I am a two-years-old."

But the tension begins to ease as they each dutifully open up the little blank booklets I've shown them how to make and begin to draw, some taking time to think, others plunging in. Their deep concentration is all that I hoped for. Except for Chika. She's absent.

❖ ❖ ❖

After the completed comic books have been passed around, admired and handed in, Chika slides in to class an hour late. The urge to shake her almost overcomes me. Heba rescues me from committing student abuse by recounting a conversation she had with her neighbor, whom she asked for help opening a stuck window. "Let's see if we can't do something about that," the neighbor says. Heba catches the gist, but, "Why he said 'can't'? Should be *can* do something."

I throw up my hands. "It's just—"

"—Interesting English," the class, in one voice, anticipates me.

"Bingo!" I say. Bing looks up, startled, from his doodles of Bugattis.

More interesting English ensues. It's always a welcome break from grammar. We dissect Jiho's puzzling idiom "piece of a cake," which he has overheard at the library in a decidedly non-culinary context: Boy to girlfriend: "I can't get this program to open." Girl (according to Jiho) to boyfriend: "Piece of a cake."

Bing then asks for help finding a famous American novel he enjoyed in China—a pirated book translated into Chinese. It spoke to his heart, and he wants to try to read it in English but can't find it on Amazon or at our local bookstore: *The Pitcher in the Rye Field.*

Ominously, though, Yumi's contribution is "spoiled child."

"What do Americans mean, 'spoiled child,'" she asks pointedly. Before I can respond, Yumi answers her own question, casting a glance in the general direction of Chika. Her voice quivers a little, as with some strong emotion—anger or anxiety. "I think 'spoiled child' means it is selfish child, does not care about other people. Because mother and father give everything." I feel a little chill. Chika is sneaking a text message and misses the jab entirely.

What is going on here? It appears that Chika's snort has been on Yumi's mind since Friday.

I've noticed that now when Chika and her boyfriend have one of their loud, jealous arguments outside the door and Chika slides into class pouting and angry, Yumi frowns, and when Yumi repeats to her the instructions that she has missed by virtue of her tardiness, Chika retorts, "You are not my grandmother."

Yumi's attentions to Chika—obliging or disapproving—seem to make no impression on Chika. Compared to the boyfriend, the freedom, the cigarettes, the greasy, salty, over-sweet American food she loves, the class and everyone in it hold no interest for her. When Yumi has given Chika the occasional piece of motivational advice, Chika takes it with bad grace. And now something has shifted. Yumi's forbearance is not just wearing thin. I think it has worn out.

·19·

THINGS ARE IMPROVING with Donna Bittner, however. The Dean of the Business School's pollen allergies have ensured that Slockett-Plum's air-conditioning has stayed cranked to the maximum. Even if Donna were tempted to show more skin, she wouldn't be able to manage it for long in such arctic conditions, and after October 1st, Iowa's autumn chill will be sufficient to keep her—a Southern California native—modestly bundled up. There will be no more complaints from mortified Muslims.

Furthermore, after the success of Byron's lecture, she seems to have assumed a whole new attitude toward teaching. By Wednesday, the last day of September, she is full of plans for bringing more speakers to her class. And now she comes to me for advice on teaching pronunciation. She hangs on my words reverentially, even taking notes.

"Wrong stress makes a speaker even less comprehensible than wrong sounds," I tell her. "If students say 'I'm having lice for lunch,' the context usually makes it obvious they're not planning to eat vermin. And if they ask for a shit of paper—" Donna looks up from the notebook and gives a shriek. "—it may be amusing, but your listeners don't assume the student was trying to be obscene. But if they stress the wrong syllable in a word or the wrong words in a sentence, the listener just gets lost."

"Like how?"

"For example, if you tell people you're taking an AERobic class—a-e-r-o-b-i-c—when you mean aeRObic, they'll inquire how your Arabic is coming along and ask you to say a few words in the language."

I'm on a roll, so I go on to explain how content words—nouns, verbs, adjectives, adverbs—get the strong beats in sentences, while function words—articles, pronouns, conjunctions—get the weak beats.

Donna is scribbling notes as fast as I can talk.

"Imagine you're planning to rob a bank. You intend to go up to the teller and say, 'Put all of your cash in the bag and keep smiling. I've got a gun.' Probably you're nervous when you get to the teller's window, and you can only manage to telegraph the content words: Put all cash bag. Keep smiling. Got gun.' Does the teller get the gist?"

Donna nods.

"But if you were to croak out only the function words—'of you in the and I've a'—the teller will ask if you're okay and would you like her to call someone for you."

"Totally awesome example!" Donna makes me repeat it while she writes it down word for word. After our meeting she signs out all the pronunciation texts from our ESL library and carries them back to her office cubicle.

So she's finally coming along, and I feel rather smug about the success of my mentoring strategies. Not nagging or micromanaging after all.

❋ ❋ ❋

After appearing at my office door Wednesday and Thursday afternoons, now at 8:30 on Monday morning before class, she enters flourishing a notepad and wearing an ingratiating smile, dimples driving deep into her pink cheeks.

"Got a minute?"

I glance at my watch. Bing is due shortly to try for the third time to understand the definite article *the* versus the indefinite *a, an*, and class starts at 9:00. Jane, I order myself, ignore the charm of the dimples!

"Oh! You're so busy! You're such a dedicated teacher." Donna puts her hand to her heart. "I'm being a pain. I'll come back later. When would be a good time?"

"Well," I say reluctantly, "I have about ten minutes now."

Donna sits briskly down in the student chair. What—she wants to know—are the pronunciation problems of Korean speakers of English and how should she handle them?

Where to begin? *r*'s and *l*'s of course, and *p*'s and *f*'s. The *zh* sound, as in television or measure. *Dzh* as in 'judge.' Syllable stress, keyword intonation ...

"How do you fix them?" Donna's pen hovers over her notebook.

"That's way beyond a ten-minute discussion. And of course you can't always 'fix' them."

"Do you have time later this afternoon?"

Just say no, Jane.

I make an appointment for 4:00 and know Donna will have me there until 5:00 or even 6:00. Here we go again. Boundaries, Jane. After this I *will* set limits.

❊ ❊ ❊

At 4:00 on the dot, Donna sets a full Café Gulp coffee mug on my desk, pulls her notebook and two pens from her big purse (now sadly missing half its rhinestones) and turns off her cell phone.

"So. Koreans," I say brusquely. Does she pick up on my irritation? I think not. "First, it's best to work on only one segmental at a time—"

"Now *what's* a segmental? I know, but I'm such an airhead today, I forget."

97

What's a segmental? How much air occupies that head for Donna to have forgotten the most basic concept in her pronunciation training?

"Vowel and consonant sounds," I say, keeping disbelief out of my voice. "As opposed to suprasegmentals, remember? The other aspects of pronunciation like rhythm and pitch?"

"Oh yeah, of course."

In the midst of a discussion of /r/ vs. /l/, Molly shuffles some papers and pushes back her office chair. It's already 5:00.

"One little trick for /z/, and then we'd better save the rest for another time," I say. Donna is on the edge of her chair. I can never resist genuine interest. "If students can't pronounce the /z/ sound as in 'easy,' have them substitute a /s/, but have them say it quickly, without emphasis, and it will sound to the listener just like a /z/." Donna tries it.

"Awesome! It works!"

"You can do the same trick with voiced affricates and the fricative /zh/. Let's think of some examples." I wait.

Donna cocks her head and bunches her lips and seems to be pondering. "I'm just drawing a blank at the moment."

Judge, language, edge, measure, usual ... I can think of a dozen examples. Donna can't come up with one?

Just then she lets her eyes fall on the wall clock.

"Your knowledge, like, really blows me away!" she cries. "Would it be horribly inconvenient for me to pick your brain again when you have more time?"

·20·

"I GUESS YOU KNOW that Dr. Stang gave another lecture to Donna Bittner's class last Friday." Ginger has run into me in the hall on Tuesday after my morning class. There's something in Ginger's tone that, as much as she is capable of harboring such a negative attitude, hints at disapproval.

"He did? No, I wasn't aware of it. That was nice of him. Rather above and beyond the call, though."

"She said she was in a jam."

According to Ginger, Donna said she wasn't feeling well on Thursday afternoon and, lest she be experiencing incipient symptoms of the dreaded H1N1 virus, asked Stang if he had a different talk he could give—spur of the moment—to fill in for her the following morning. And yet she met with *me* at 4:00 on Thursday, kept me there until after 5:00 and seemed her perky self.

Ginger purses her lips in an un-Ginger-like expression. "Donna kind of heaped on the praise about his first lecture."

I can imagine.

"Well," I say, "we don't want to take advantage of his good nature. I'll have a chat with Donna about it. I hadn't realized she was sick. She seemed fine on Thursday afternoon. But anyway, she should have asked one of our teachers to fill in."

❊ ❊ ❊

99

Donna's "brain-picking" session that afternoon is devoted to Japanese pronunciation difficulties—the Japanese habit of pronouncing every alphabetic letter *a* as *ah* ("mop" for "map"), every voiced *th* as *z* ("zot" for "that"), and voiceless *th* as *s* ("sahnk you" for "thank you). There were some English words Japanese students should be warned about (the correct pronunciation of letter *a* in "fact" and the letters *ee* in sheet"). Donna takes thorough notes and thanks me, as always, profusely.

"By the way," I say, "if you get sick or have a doctor's appointment, come to one of us to sub for you. It's not really appropriate to ask someone outside the Program to do it."

Donna widens her already rather over-wide eyes, giving her an astonished marmoset expression.

"You mean Dr. Stang? Oh wow, I'm sorry! I just thought you all were so busy and … you know," she lowers her voice, "I thought it might boost his confidence. He's *such* a good teacher, but he's *so* insecure."

✵ ✵ ✵

Ignoring, for once, her unruly headscarf, Heba, with a pink glow on her olive cheeks, announces that she is "very exciting—" I surmise to myself that there are several in the room who would agree with her there. "—about good news! Because I am accepting to the Medical School at the University of Iowa when I am finished English."

"You've been accept*ed*? Congratulations! And this," I wait for the applause to die down, "is the perfect opportunity to review our passive adjectives: What is 'exciting'—Heba? Or Heba's news?"

Heba's *news*, they agree.

Heba lifts her chin haughtily. As I have mentioned, she is the oldest in her family and is used to mercilessly bullying her twenty-one year-old younger brother, here at McBee. Under her supervision, Mohammed is not allowed to watch television until he finishes his

English homework. Heba is not one to take correction without an argument.

"'I am exciting' it's correct!" she declares.

"Is it?" I ask the group. "Heba is excit- …?"

"—*ted*," says Yumi.

"—*ted*?" Heba frowns.

Guillermo can't let this pass.

"For me, for Ted, for anyone," he says, "Heba also is excit*ing*."

It takes a beat before Heba gets it. She raises an eyebrow at him. "Heba is engaged for marry," she says severely.

"Then," replies Guillermo, pantomiming tear drops falling down his cheeks, "I am disappointing."

"Disappoint*ing*?" Heba glances at me archly.

"Disappoint*ed*!" correct the others in unison.

"All right," I say, thinking of the two-hour sexual harassment prevention training the staff was made to endure last spring, "time to move on."

* * *

The McBee ESL students are going on a field trip to a farm and corn maze on the weekend, and on Friday I advise them to wear layers. "If it turns out to be warm, you can always leave your coat on the bus."

Jiho The Question Man's hand is in the air at once. "Why you said, 'always'? Always mean forever. I leave my jacket on bus forever? It's not make sense."

How to explain "always" in this context?

"'Always' doesn't mean forever in this sentence. In this situation it's a set expression. It means something like 'in that case.'"

"Too many meanings," Jiho grumbles. "How I can remember all of those?"

The answer? You can't. Don't worry about it. But he does worry. They all worry. At the end of the semester, they will take the dreaded

Test of English as a Foreign Language—TOEFL. The TOEFL listening section is full of mean little items like "You can always leave your coat on the bus" with the accompanying question, "What does the speaker imply?"

It is an overcast morning, and the students' eyes start to glaze over as I introduce future *when*-clauses with the simple present aspect. The day is cold, but Bing, bare-armed in a T-shirt ("Voldemort Rules" stretched across his round torso), looks hot and sleepy in the overheated classroom, and I think a song, "She'll Be Coming 'Round the Mountain When She Comes," might revive everybody and teach the grammar point at the same time.

I ask the students to create alternative lyrics to the tune played on the CD player.

Winking at Mi-young, Guillermo sings, "He'll Be Looking Pretty Happy When She Comes." Mi-young's sly response, "She'll Be Wearing Lot of Diamond When She Goes," elicits general laughter.

Inserting percussion into the proceedings, Guillermo pulls off his backward facing cap and keeps time by slapping it against his thigh. Masoud, too, starts to clap out the rhythm. Heba, Mariam, and even Fiesta nod their heads in unison, and Jiho taps on his desktop with his retractable pencil. Bing stomps one foot, without much sense of rhythm, but with verve, and Won, breaking his silence, drums on the metal lid of his electronic dictionary.

When Yumi's turn comes, her verse, "I'll Be Buying Three Potatoes When I Shop," is quickly taken up. The song ends with a triumphant, ornamental flourish by the drummers.

Chika fails to contribute a verse—"I can't *think* of anything," she insists. She watches, irritated, from her seat by the door. It's a minute past the time for the break, and she's eager to get out in the hall to resume her latest fight with Allen/Aaron. But Yumi says, "Wait," and asks the others, coyly, "I think something wrong with my song."

Guillermo kisses his fingers at her. "No! Is perfect!"

Spontaneously, in a quavering soprano, Yumi tries a new version: "I'll Be Keeping Track of Budget While I Shop."

"Yumi, I pay you one hundred dollars, you give me special lesson after class!" exclaims Guillermo, pretending to fish in his pockets for money. Apologizing and thanking, a flush of pleasure brightening her battered old face, Yumi begins to sit down again. Suddenly, from her seat by the door, Chika heaves a gigantic sigh—more audible by far than any of the many sighs she is famous for. In a loud, sullen voice, and looking directly at me, she says, "Who *cares*!" and stalks out of the room.

"Hey!" shouts Guillermo, good-naturedly. "Be polite!"

The others tut tut, shaking their heads a little, and, humming the tune to "She'll Be Coming 'Round the Mountain," meander out to the restrooms and drinking fountain.

Yumi doesn't move. At Chika's affront to me, she sits frozen in her chair. On her face is an expression I have never seen there before, a look of hatred that twists her mouth as if she tastes something bitter. What has become of her "too happy" glow? Chika has robbed her of it. Damned spoiled brat! They should tell her grandmother to come and haul Chika back to Japan and marry her off. I almost say it aloud.

I shock myself with the nastiness of the thought. It makes me ashamed and uneasy. And before I can figure out what to say to Yumi, she has slipped silently out of the classroom.

·21·

*A*FTER HER RUDE OUTBURST, Chika returns to class in a good mood, apparently having made up with her boyfriend during the break. Yumi is quiet and preoccupied and doesn't look at Chika during the whole period.

It's high time to take control of the situation. I cannot sacrifice the cheer of Yumi and the rest of the class to this young woman's sulks and self-indulgence. Chika's behavior is insulting and disruptive. Instead of childishly despising her, I must, absolutely, sit her down and have a talk with her about "Who *cares*!" and all the other remarks like it.

Having made up my mind, I find my opportunity toward the end of the period, when the students are absorbed in working individually on a writing exercise.

I walk resolutely to Chika's seat by the door. Her head is bent over her work, her tongue protruding a little and her long legs twined tightly around each other as she moves her pen on the page. The pose suddenly brings up a memory of my brother's younger daughter on the day we went to pick her up after her first morning at kindergarten. When we had left three hours earlier, Audrey's tragic little face was turned back toward her father and me, her chin just starting to crumple and her eyes filling with tears. When we returned at noon, Audrey was sitting at a big table, wielding a crayon on a piece of newsprint. She sat in just such a rapt pose as Chika did now, completely absorbed, with her tongue pressed against her upper lip.

Chika doesn't notice me, so I can see her paper, filled with borders and flourishes and in one corner a skillful caricature of her boyfriend. Chika's nail-bitten fingers move the pen in confident strokes as she sketches the hollows of the boyfriend's cheeks and the long pointed chin, not neglecting the conspicuous Adam's apple under it, which makes his spindly neck look like a snake half way through the gurgitation of a small rodent. I stand watching her silently for some moments, and then, unable to rebuke her, move on to help another student.

* * *

Every Friday afternoon, there being no mosque in Zenith, classes are suspended so the Muslim students can carpool to Des Moines for afternoon prayer. I am only teaching two classes this semester instead of three because I have a course release to work on revising the Program's curriculum objectives, so I look forward to these quiet Friday afternoon interludes—the chance to catch up on the curriculum work and finish my grading.

After my week's anxiety over Chika and Yumi, the sardines and crackers I've brought for lunch sound unappetizing and uncomforting. I decide to buy a treat from Slockett-Plum's opulent food kiosk, bring it back to my office and sit down for a good think.

I'm standing in line at the kiosk when I'm tapped painfully on the shoulder and turn to find the nasty little watery blue eyes, cauliflower nose and coarse, ruddy complexion of Geology Department despot Gus Tamerius aggressively close to my face. He is in one of his expansive moods and booms at me, apropos of nothing, "You sure got your work cut out for you over there!"

I'm never sure if Tamerius knows my name even after almost twenty-five years across the hall from him. I pull back several inches.

"My work—?"

"With those clueless foreign students of yours."

"Excuse me?"

"How do you get through to 'em when they have no idea what you're saying?"

"Well, they *do* have some idea. Their English proficiency depends on—"

"Not the ones your buxom colleague got me to talk to today. Fucking zombies. Deer in the headlights." He passes a hand back and forth in front of his face to illustrate their cluelessness. An Asian student in line ahead of us turns to glance at Tamerius. "Not a peep out of 'em. I finally just held up specimens and pointed. 'Fossil.' 'Meteorite.' 'Moon rock.'"

"*Whose* class was this?"

"Christ, I don't know—Dina, Dinah, something with a D—"

"Donna?"

"Yeah. Donna somebody. I wouldn't have done it if I'd known what I was getting in for. My advice—be sure she sticks around to translate. How many languages do you all speak over there?"

"Donna wasn't in the class?"

"Hell, no. She said they're supposed to experience university classes without an English teacher to hold their hand. But my opinion is you're jumping the gun with these people—Goddamn it! Out of latté *again*?!" The Asian student ahead of us has come away from the kiosk's coffee cart empty-handed, and Tamerius pushes past me to shout at the work-study student staffing the cart. I decide to settle for sardines and crackers after all, and walk briskly back to the office.

At the office I poke my head into Donna's cubicle, but Donna, her coat, and the big leather purse are not there. I ask if anyone has seen Donna Bittner today. No one has. It's Friday, so, without afternoon classes, she's managed to take the whole day off.

※ ※ ※

"I gather you have a regular lecture series going," I say to Donna on Monday, having snagged her and herded her into my office just as she's leaving.

"Oh, yeah. It's great," she says, "thanks to your awesome advice."

"Well, I'm glad it's going okay, but—"

"The students are completely into it!"

"—but *you* need to attend the lectures so you can discuss them with the students afterwards."

"Oh, I attend them."

"*All* of them?"

"Um, I think so. Well, I might have missed one, but that was on purpose. I—"

"Are you testing the students over the contents of the lectures?"

"Mm hm." Donna turns to gaze at the top row of books on my bookshelf.

"Why don't I take a look at the tests you've given so far, and the distribution of scores. Testing can be tricky."

Donna pulls a book from my shelf. "I've read this! It's so good."

"I have some time right now. Let's take a look at your tests together."

But it seems Donna hasn't actually typed up and printed her tests. She decided it made more sense to write the questions on the board, to save on printing and paper, she asserts (Kaye having complained at the last staff meeting about overuse of the copy machine). "I think she was really right about that," declares Donna. "We should start thinking outside the box about conserving paper."

I invite myself to the next lecture Donna has lined up. When is it scheduled? The details are still being worked out. Donna will let me know.

"Are your lectures a Friday morning activity?"

"Sometimes. I think it makes, like, a great end to the week. Something different the students can look forward to."

Donna's comment at the beginning of the semester about lack of technology in her original classroom comes back to me—"I can't play DVDs or go on YouTube"—and I wonder, now that Donna is in Slockett-Plum, what does she do with DVDs and YouTube? Start a movie and just stick her students in front of it like a busy parent pawning her children off on Saturday morning cartoons?

·22·

P ASSING THE OPEN Geology Department door before lunch on Thursday, I greet Gretchen Pettit with a habitual "good morning," not expecting a reply, but Gretchen, ignoring a ringing phone, calls back, "The Geology Department has enough to do without teaching your ESL classes for you."

"Excuse me?"

Somehow, Donna has gotten past the Pettit portcullis into the inner sanctum of Professor Bloss's lab and lined up the overworked assistant professor to give a lecture for that Friday. Heaven knows how she's managed it. Perhaps she followed him into the restroom.

I trade classes with Molly again on Friday and drop in on Donna's class. Dr. Bloss gives quite a good lecture, but only half of Donna's students attend. There's no one to take roll and there will be no quiz.

Molly, it turns out, was also enlisted to sub for Donna on a Friday morning earlier in October, due to an unspecified "family emergency." Another ESL teacher, three months' pregnant and still throwing up in the restroom on a regular basis, reveals that she, too, has filled in for Donna on two separate Fridays because of a dental appointment and a "car emergency."

✳ ✳ ✳

One thing you can say for Donna, she's an organizer. With no classes on Friday afternoons (the Muslims all in Des Moines for communal prayer) and the lecture series or substitute teachers on Friday mornings, she has managed to organize herself half a semester of three-day week-ends at McBee U.'s expense.

It's going to make me look bad, but I can't keep this to myself. I go directly to Kaye Bibber's office.

"Kaye," I confess, "there's a problem. It's my fault." Kaye gestures me to a chair, but I'm too perturbed to sit. "The red flags were waving all over the place, but I just felt stymied by Donna's slipperiness, and I was afraid of micromanaging—I have that tendency—" Kaye raises an eyebrow. "—but I should have been more hands on. And now—although I *will* say that at least Donna's been conscientious about teaching pronunciation. She's asked for my advice about the Koreans, and just today she asked about Japanese and Arab pronunciation problems, but ..."

After Kaye firmly sits me down and gets me to stop babbling and come out with the essentials, we agree that it's time that we speak to Donna together.

❊ ❊ ❊

Donna is both abject and imaginative in her apologies and excuses.

"Oh my God, I'm soo soo sorry! I should have asked what the policy was! I was thinking it would be *good* for me not to be at the lectures. Like giving the students more independence and treating them more like adults? But if you say it's unacceptable, I'm totally fine with following whatever rules there are here. I think it's really important to be a team player!"

As to her leaning too heavily on colleagues in Linguistics and Geology, she is "a little dumbfounded" to hear this. Professor Tamerius and Professor Stang had seemed kind of flattered to be asked, and she thought Professor Bloss might feel hurt if she asked Tamerius and didn't ask him, too. But if she had realized they were off limits...!

"It was actually Jane who suggested the lecture series,"—Not every week! I open my mouth to protest— "but I wouldn't dream of imposing on those guys again now that you've made the rules clear!"

＊ ＊ ＊

On Monday in Low Intermediate Grammar/Writing I introduce the notoriously misused quantifiers *little, a little, few,* and *a few.* Masoud is the first to write his sentence on the blackboard: "*When I start work at Des Moines Sanicorp I had little friends. Now I have friends Pascual, Luis, Truong, Korfa, and Jerry.*"

"Thank you, Masoud." I turn to the others. "So how many friends did Masoud have when he start*ed* work at Sanicorp?"

"No much," answers Guillermo. "Lonely guy!"

"Fiesta? What do you think?"

It occurs to me that I might have to administer the Heimlich maneuver to dislodge the sentence caught in Fiesta's throat. But at last she coughs it up. "Two, or one friend?"

"Good! Is that what you meant, Masoud?"

"Yes! One friend, maybe two, but not even real friend, just we say, 'Hi.'"

"So we understand what you mean because you gave us a *context* for your first sentence. Your second sentence—" I point to it. "—explains that *now* you have five friends. Different from before. But, Masoud, erase your second sentence and let's look at the first one alone."

Masoud erases the sentence and stands back.

"What do you mean by this sentence: '*When I started . . .*' (I can't resist correcting the verb tense again.) '*. . . work at Des Moines Sanicorp, I had little friends.*'"

Masoud frowns. "Something wrong about my words?" He studies the sentence for some seconds.

"Can anyone help Masoud?"

Bing mouths the words in the sentence. Won rapidly thumbs through the textbook.

Yumi raises her hand. When I acknowledge her, she pushes aside her great wheeled backpack and walks silently to the board.

"Excuse me. I'm sorry," she says, dropping little bows toward Masoud and me and the class at large. Under Masoud's sentence, she draws a stick figure. This tall stick figure she labels "Masoud." Two tiny stick figures next to it at ankle height she labels, "Little Friends."

Masoud throws back his head and laughs.

Guillermo claps and whistles. "Yumi, you're artist!" She shakes her head and with modest demurrals hurries back to her seat.

"So why can't we use '*little*' in this context?" I ask when the noise subsides.

"Masoud don't use *little* for *small* meaning—"

"He mean *almost no friend*."

"So what word do you need, Masoud?"

"Few friends?"

"Exactly. Why?"

"Because … *friends* you can count? It's count noun? Use *few* with count noun. *Little* with uncount noun."

"That's right. So your mistake helped us understand the difference. Thank you."

"But I have better sentence!" Masoud exclaims.

On the blackboard he writes, "First time, my Sanicorp friends know little knowledge about my country and verse vica. But now we know."

I let *know knowledge* and *verse vica* pass. "That's it! 'Knowledge' is noncount, so you used '*little*'!" Masoud smiles with satisfaction. Guillermo shakes his hand as he passes on his way back to his seat.

Chika's eyes are closed, her backpack serving as a convenient pillow.

Looking down at the top of her head, her bleached hair hanging straw-like across her backpack, I think, the nerve! I tap her sharply on the shoulder.

"Rise and shine, Sleeping Beauty."

She looks up blearily. "I'm not sleep," she says.

As she's getting out the door at the end of class, I stop her. I've made up my mind to go for one last try before giving up.

"Chika, be in my office this afternoon at 3:00. Do not be late."

She gives me that wide-eyed open-mouthed indignant look— What did *I* do? But apparently she registers the set of my mouth and the anger in my eyes. Perhaps she sees her grandmother's face. She comes at 3:00.

❊ ❊ ❊

By the time she arrives, I've calmed down and had time to think.

Okay, I wasted my time with the comic book exercise, the idiom essay didn't work out, but I'm going to assume that somewhere in that convoluted cortex of hers there is a smidgeon of tissue that can feel empathy. I sit her down.

"Chika, we're going to try a little experiment." She waits, incuriously. "You're going to be the teacher, and I'm going to be the student."

"What you mean?"

I close the door. "Go stand by the door."

"Why?"

"Just do it." I say it sharply. She drags herself over to the door. I take a seat on Molly's chair, which is by the window, farthest from Chika. "We'll pretend that you're the teacher and you're standing in front of the classroom. I am a student in your class. You are going to teach me something for a few minutes."

She screws up her nose. "Teach what? I'm not teacher."

She can't, or wouldn't, talk for even half a minute about gram-

113

mar or her experiences at McBee or her family or her boyfriend.
I've anticipated this.

"I want you to tell the story of a movie that you like a lot—"

"I don't know a movie."

I know for a fact that she's a fan of Japanese anime.

"Tell me about your favorite anime movie."

"Anime? You mean cartoon movie?"

"Yes. What's your favorite?"

She ponders this for a few seconds, then, grudgingly ... *Ponyo*.
But you won't like. You're old woman. It's for young."

"That's your teaching job, to make me interested in the movie
even though I'm not young. Explain what's great about this ... what
is it? *Ponyo*?" She nods. "And while you're explaining, I'm going to
listen to you in one way. And then I'll listen to you in another way."

"What way?"

"You'll see. Just do it. Start. Now."

"Just tell about movie?"

"Yes. What about the movie interests you most and why."

Her hands hang listlessly at her sides as she begins.

"*Ponyo* wins many prize in Japan. *Ponyo* is famous. Everyone
love *Ponyo*."

"Not just young people?"

"Well, maybe every kind of people."

"Why?"

"Because it has beautiful expression. Not just cartoon, but also
art." Her hands lose their lethargy. "All pictures are draw by hands,
not computer. Artists make many pictures for movie." Her finger
traces numerals on her palm. She takes a pen from my desk, writes
the number and holds it out for me.

"A hundred and seventy *thousand* drawings?!"

"Yes. So many. All pictures draw by hands! Old-fashioned way."

"Wow, that's impressive."

"And music very good. Everyone love *Ponyo* music. There's famous cute song by child. Nozomi Ohashi sings that song. She's eight year old."

"Can you sing it for me?"

With no self-consciousness, Chika sings the song in a little girl soprano and using hand gestures. Chika can sing!

"That was sweet. I liked it. The movie sounds interesting. Is there an English language version that I could watch?"

"Yes, but they say Japanese names in English way. Sounds weird."

I let silence fall for a few seconds.

"Okay, Chika. Now why don't you tell me a little about the story of the movie. What is the movie about?"

"It's about goldfish lives in the sea. Her father is wizard. She have magic power. But she comes out of sea by accident and little boy, Sosuke, save her …"

Should I carry out what I've planned? I hate to spoil her enthusiasm. But that's the point, isn't it? To put her in other people's shoes?

As she tells the story, I slump in my chair and idly study my nails. I sigh and look out the window. I jiggle my foot. After a bit, she stops talking and stands there, her expression blank. I sit up.

"So Chika, what did you notice about how I listened to you the first time and how I listened just now?"

She shrugs. "First way look interested. Second way not interest."

"What made you think I wasn't interested, the second way?"

She shakes her head. "Just you don't look at me."

"And how did it feel to teach when your student seemed uninterested? No, first, how did it feel when I listened with interest?"

"It's okay."

"And the second way?"

"Second way was real way. Because you don't interest in young movie. First way is fake way."

"No!" I get up. "I really was interested, *both* times. But you see

115

what it feels like to stand before a class and see a student who looks bored and—"

She shakes her head.

"You want me to listen to grammar lesson in fake way?"

"No, Chika, but ..." I'm at a loss. "At least show some courtesy, politeness," I say feebly. "Don't you see how rude it is to—" I've ended up lecturing like her grandmother.

She looks at her watch. "Can I go? I'm late."

My, Jane, that was effective.

·23·

I'S JUST AFTER MIDTERM and Kaye calls me in to ask about Chika's progress in Grammar and Writing.

"She's doing abysmally. D's in both, and that's a gift. In Reading, too, according to Molly."

Kaye informs me that Chika's mother has sent a request to see her daughter's midterm grades.

"You let her know Chika had to give permission?"

Kaye sighs. "Yes, there was the usual outrage, 'I'm her mother! I pay her fees'!"

"The mother wrote that herself? In English?"

"I'd guess she had an English speaker do it."

"Chika won't be too keen on giving permission."

"Well, it's between her and her mother. But in case she does give her permission, can you give me her grades officially, in writing?"

I promise to e-mail them to her.

The next day Chika comes to my office demanding to know her current course grade. I enlighten her.

"But I must get high grade because my mother asked to Kaye my grade, and she can't get grade information except I write a note it's okay. Permission note."

"Yes, that's right. Did Kaye explain it? You're nineteen, so you're legally an adult. Your grade is private. Even your parents can't see it without your permission. That's a law in this country. It's called

117

FERPA—Family Education Rights and Privacy Act. It means *all* your educational information is private."

Chika flops gloomily into the student chair. "If no note, my mother stops to send money. No money, I must back to Japan. But if my mother sees low grade, I back to Japan also. I need increase grade!" She frowns at me. "Why you give me D? Donna give A and her class is higher class."

"Well, you must have demonstrated a higher skill in Communication Skills than in Grammar and Writing. Or Reading."

What, I wonder, are Donna's grading criteria? Does she just hand out A's to everyone? Chika answers the unstated question.

"In Donna's class there have no tests. Just I must talk in class every day to get A. In Donna's class correctly speak is no matter. Fluently is matter. I think Donna's class is better way." Should I rat Donna out about her grade inflation? But the teachers have already been warned about it. Kaye will see it at the end of the semester when grades are submitted to the Registrar. And I've already had to lean on Kaye over Donna's revealing clothes and the lecture series. Leave it alone, Jane. Don't micromanage.

"I should go to *GET IN!* school. In there I pass TOEFL soon." As if Chika had the discipline to memorize the answers to those thousands of sample test items.

"Well, why don't you?"

"If I go away from McBee, my grandmother make me come home. Aaron is here."

* * *

By Tuesday, Yumi's animosity toward Chika has increased to the point that she scolds Chika outright for her failure to bring her book to class and glares at the hovering boyfriend for being in the way when she leaves the classroom. This is not like Yumi. What is going on?

A kind of warfare has risen up between the two Japanese. Is it just generational? Yet Yumi is kind and tolerant of Bing's lack of diligence, Fiesta's reluctance to speak, Guillermo's silliness, even Jiho's frequent interruptions to ask questions. These students are as young as Chika. Yumi must be angry with Chika for a different reason. Was it that "Who cares!" remark of Chika's that tipped the balance? Her blatant disrespect for a teacher? I should have chastised Chika for it. It was only cowardice, or maybe hurt pride on my own part that made me prefer to ignore the remark.

On Friday, Chika is absent, indulging in one of her three-day weekends. Yumi brings out her ubiquitous camera, though she has taken pictures of the class not five days earlier. Rather glumly, she rounds everyone up for another group shot and ignores Guillermo's, "Yumi, you are like paparazzi!"

✳ ✳ ✳

On the weekend, my siblings call from the East and West Coasts respectively to invite me for Thanksgiving next month. Several of the nieces and nephews will be home for the holiday, and, to take advantage of lower rates, they exhort me to get my ticket early. The thought of air travel on that brief four-day weekend is too daunting, and I decline with thanks. I'll accept a local friend's open invitation to spend the holiday with her extended family. But the phone calls from my brother and sister leave me feeling sad and disconnected.

Now I walk around the house picking up and putting down the various family photos that stand on mantelpiece and shelves. I gaze for several minutes at a black and white photo from a Colorado vacation my family took in the 1950s. Three little pup tents and my parents' large tent in the background. I can almost smell the musty army surplus sleeping bags and remember the quiet voices of my parents talking outside at the picnic table as I drift into sleep. *You were so happy child*, Yumi had said, wistfully. Yes, I was a happy child. What about her? Is there a reason Yumi can so easily be turned glum by Chika?

Aloud, I lament, "Yumi, how can I cheer you up?" I'm at a loss.

·24·

ON MONDAY AFTER CLASSES, several young Japanese women students are bellied up to Doug Best's reception counter imbibing deep drafts of his intoxicating presence when his Brazilian wife Rosa breezes into the office with the clumber spaniels on leashes. Doug's admirers quickly abandon him for the dogs.

"No one can resist the clumbers," says Rosa in her sultry Brazilian-Portuguese accented English.

The puppies, Sheryl and Sue, have grown since August, when Doug showed me their background photo on his computer, but they haven't grown into their feet. Doug insists clumbers were bred in England to hunt, but, really, how do creatures with such short legs and dragging ears run down prey? Maybe the foxes stop in their tracks to stare at them in stupefaction.

"We got girls because we didn't want them marking the neighbors' trash cans."

Ah, Doug Best—always considerate of others, and so gorgeous, to boot.

The admiring young women now kneel beside Sheryl and Sue, stroke their silky white mud-tipped ears and freckled muzzles and make Japanese cooing noises. Rosa has brought the clumbers to the office to show off the costumes the dogs will wear to a Halloween party: Harley Davidson-brand reflective collars with the words "Bad to the Bone."

"They'll be going as bikers," Rosa explains.

❊ ❊ ❊

But when Rosa takes the clumbers home, she gets word that her father has had a stroke, and they aren't sure if he's going to make it. She has been summoned to Brazil as fast as she can get there. Doug will go with her.

I'm not much of a dog person, but I can't resist Doug's soulful eyes and those thick lashes, and I do have a fenced yard, so I volunteer to look after Sheryl and Sue while he and Rosa fly to Rio.

❊ ❊ ❊

That evening it takes us five trips to and from Doug's van to unload Sheryl's and Sue's paraphernalia: not only dog food but treats for good behavior, two commodious plush dog beds, stainless steel bowls monogrammed with "$\mathcal{S}$" in Gothic font, brushes, leashes, plastic bags for walk time waste disposal, a ball flinger, squeaking toys of every description, and more. I am starting to fully realize the task I've taken on.

Sheryl and Sue stand in the yard panting and drooling excitedly while the contents of the van are unloaded and brought into the kitchen.

"Be sure to put their beds side by side." Doug looks down at the dogs with adoration in those liquid brown eyes (his, not theirs). "They like separate beds, but they like to sleep in each other's faces. And they love their toys, don't you, girls? If they hear, 'Time for bed,' they'll run and find a toy to sleep with. If someone comes over and they start to jump on them, just say, 'Nice hello!' and they'll sit down. Then give them a cheese square."

Doug runs over a list of detailed instructions on their feeding schedule.

"I hope I haven't forgotten anything." He does a final inventory and gives me the vet's cell phone number.

At last he opens the kitchen door, on which Sheryl and Sue have been pressing their moist, rust-pink rubbery noses, leaving a line of smudges, and goes outside. On the back patio he lowers his tall frame to kneel by the clumbers and let them lick his face. Then with backward apologetic looks (to them, not me) and baby talk endearments, he gets in his van, thanks me, and regretfully drives off.

For a few moments Sheryl and Sue stare through the fence at the place where the van was parked, then turn with tongue-lolling grins toward me, bound over and jump with muddy forepaws on my new down coat from L. L. Bean.

"*Nice* hello!" I command, too late. They sit obediently and wait for cheese.

I bring them in and towel off their feet, after which they nose around the kitchen, lapping up crumbs and sniffing at corners. Eventually, they plop down on the linoleum and pant up at me, waiting for the good times and the cheese squares to roll. I feel a little claustrophobic. Is this what it's like to have children? You can't ever just ignore them and go your way? I never had much interest in having children and rather enjoy my self-sufficient life. My brief marriage to a controlling man dampened what little incentive I may have had to embark on another man quest. So having any living being dependent on me is unsettling. Still, two temporary dogs are not going to deprive me of my independence.

❊ ❊ ❊

I open the back door and they trot outside, their feathery white tails swishing behind them like conductors' wands. They turn to look back as I shut the door, and their foreheads ripple upward, pulling at the base of their ears with a look of extreme surprise as if to say, "How very odd. She's staying inside?"

I feel guilty. Probably I should play with them a little. I change into a worn pea coat and jeans, dig the Chuck-It ball flinger out of the dog toy chest, and slip one of their yellow tennis balls into my pocket.

The dogs are already busy snuffling around the yard. They come racing over when they hear the door open, their white ears streaming backwards like the headgear on The Flying Nun.

Their fluffy hind ends bounce over the hosta beds as the ball soars past them. The Chuck-It makes me feel almost athletic. My aim begins to improve.

Later, I take the beds, dishes, and toy box to the spare bedroom in the basement and bring Sheryl and Sue down to introduce them to their new home. They promptly pull their tug-of-war rope out of the box and wrangle over it with great ferocity until, alarmed, I hold the two rawhide bagels in their faces, upon which they drop the rope and hunker down side by side for a companionable nosh. Dog care. It's a cross cultural experience.

✻ ✻ ✻

Before my radio alarm goes off on Tuesday, I wake to a sound—coming though the heat vent—like a rush-hour traffic jam of irritable elf drivers laying on horns. Strewn underfoot on the basement stairs and all about the bedroom are squeak toys. Sheryl, treading on her squeaking fleece slipper, is at the same time trying to break the neck of a squeaking Mr. Bill. A squeaking tennis ball protrudes from one side of Sue's mouth and a squeaking frog from the other. This is what is known as a wake-up call.

I go back upstairs to prepare their breakfast. Ordinarily I begin my day listening to Chopin piano etudes.

·25·

IN SPITE OF THE chastisement in Kaye's office, Donna takes another Friday off. No lecture this time. Instead, for Friday, October 30th, she has assigned her students to spend the class time walking around campus asking American students about the Halloween tradition. There's nothing wrong with the activity in and of itself (although it should have been assigned as homework), but I wonder how much, if any, preparation Donna has given her students for the task: what polite language to use in approaching a stranger to ask a question, how to explain the purpose of the assignment, what specific questions to ask, and so forth. Will they write a report of these interviews and present them to the class? Or is this just busy work?

When I go to Donna's office at noon to ask about the assignment, she isn't there and her computer is shut down. She appears not to be coming back—if she has come in at all. I also notice that the pronunciation books from the ESL library aren't on her desk, her bookshelf, or returned to the library shelves. Donna has apparently taken them home to study over the weekend. Well, good.

❋ ❋ ❋

On Monday, just after everyone arrives and is seated, Yumi, bowing and apologizing to me for delaying class, hurries from desk to desk to distribute the complimentary prints of the photos she took in class on Friday.

When she draws near Chika's seat, Chika reaches out desultorily and plucks the last print from Yumi's hand. Without missing a beat, Yumi seizes Chika by the wrist and snatches the picture back. "No," she says severely. "You not in these photograph. You are absent Friday. You can't have picture." Then she abruptly retires to her seat and shoves the extra photo in her book bag.

I'm too stunned to be aware that I'm staring until Yumi looks up with the same bitter and distorted expression that was on her face after Chika's "Who *cares!*" remark. Now the hatred on Yumi's face dissolves into confusion as she notices me looking at her. She hurriedly opens her grammar book and obscures her face behind it, but a film of sweat on her forehead has moistened her bangs.

For the rest of the period Yumi does not meet my eyes. She seems withdrawn from her classmates, too, and at the end of the hour hurries away, beating even Chika to the door.

❊ ❊ ❊

During the first week of November, everybody seems brought down by Yumi's odd lack of cheer, everybody except Chika, who is neither more nor less disengaged than usual. Mi-young asks Yumi if she has a headache, but Yumi says, no, she's just "tired a little" and makes an effort to rally, but it isn't the real thing—not the enthusiasm we've all come to expect of her.

Their other teacher, too, is noticing something awry.

"Jane!" Molly Askew-Ohashi pulls her earbuds out when I come into our office. Molly grades papers to music so loud I can hear it tinkling from across the room. "What's happened to Yumi Murata's glow? She sits in class like she's on a death watch. Is she sick?"

"I don't know. It started after she had a couple of altercations with Chika Yamamoto. But it has to be more than that."

"Yeah, I noticed they don't seem to get along. How come? Do you know? Yumi's usually so nice to everyone, regardless."

Clearly it's my fault. I'm the one who left Yumi vulnerable to Chika's hostility.

"I think she's offended by Chika's rudeness to me," I reply. "I can't figure out how to handle the situation."

"Oh, it's probably just mid-term slump," says Molly, kindly. "She'll get over it."

"Yes. It's probably just that."

* * *

But my conscience tells me it's time to confess to Kaye. I sit in her office disconsolately.

"I feel like a failure with Chika, Kaye. Nothing I do helps."

Kaye is, predictably, both firm and reassuring.

"Jane, you've taught long enough to know better. We'll always have unmotivated students beyond our control. You can't reach everybody."

"But, you know, I can sympathize with her. She isn't a student who can sit still in a classroom. She's an artist."

Kaye pats the back of my hand maternally. She's five years younger than I am, but I appreciate the gesture.

"Jane, there comes a time when we have to let a student sink or swim. You've done your best. Let it go."

* * *

After my talk with Kaye, I hurry home on the bus to take care of the dogs. I feel a bit hemmed in, bound by clockwork to creatures with needs only I can satisfy.

As soon as I get home, I let them out and am relieved to see that without obvious urgency they take a few minutes to explore the backyard before doing their business. The squirrels who inhabit the yard peevishly chitter at the dog invasion, and I think they take some satisfaction in making Sheryl and Sue dizzy with a game of keep-away around the broad trunk of the oak. After a few rounds of this game, I bring the clumbers back in, towel them off and feed them.

That evening I lay a fire in my fireplace and pull the easy chair up close. I gaze for a long time at the flaming hardwood logs and their glowing undersides. I wonder what sort of life Yumi has lived up to now. What made her confess, "Whole my life was very bad time"? She mentioned once having worked in a factory, spray painting bento boxes. Was it boredom that Jesus had saved her from? Or memories of some kind of abuse?

The logs are gradually consumed and the blaze dies to embers. I stir them briefly with the poker but don't have the will to fetch more logs from the garage. I let the fire go out. The dogs have fallen asleep at my feet.

❖ ❖ ❖

On Monday, Mi-young confesses a serious problem which has troubled her all week-end. A man bothered her at the bus stop when she was waiting to go back to the dorm on Friday afternoon. She quickly moved away, but now she's afraid to wait there for the bus.

"What did he do?" Too late, I wonder if we ought to discuss it in private.

The man had come up to Mi-young and said, "Do you have time?"

"'Do you have time?' Those were his exact words?"

His exact words. Mi-young is certain.

What else had he said? Nothing, only that. And were there other people around? Yes, there were several people there. Did he touch her? No, he didn't touch her.

"Okay," I reply. "I'm going to say two sentences, and I want you to listen and tell me if they're the same sentence or different sentences. Are you ready?" The others lean forward and, along with Mi-young, close their eyes, the better to concentrate. "Here they are. Sentence 1: 'Do you have time?' Sentence 2: 'Do you have the time?' Same? Raise your hands if you think so."

Mi-young's, Jiho's, Won's, Fiesta's and Bing's hands all go up.

"Different?" Mariam, Heba, Yumi, Masoud, and Guillermo raise theirs. Chika abstains. I say the sentences again, more slowly, 'Do you have time?' 'Do you have the time?' and the first group makes "Oohh!" sounds. Not *time* but *the* time. The definite article.

"That guy just ask her what time is it," Chika sneers, holding up the large Mickey Mouse watch on her wrist. "No big deal."

"I ran away from him!" exclaims Mi-young, laughing. "He will think I am crazy!"

"It's not *you're* crazy," declares Masoud, "It's *English* crazy. Always '*the*,' '*a*,' '*an*.' You even can't hear them! And sometimes *no* article. How you can know? In Kiswahili article isn't necessary."

Yumi contributes nothing to the discussion, not even to contradict Masoud on his characterization of English as "crazy" rather than "interesting."

At lunch, although it isn't Yumi's regular Bible study day, I see her in the cafeteria with the young woman of the puffed sleeves and silver cross. With downcast eyes, Yumi is listening intently and rubbing her thumb back and forth along the gilt edge of her closed Bible, nodding occasionally. Several times they open the book together, and the young woman flips efficiently through the pages until she finds a passage, which she touches for emphasis. Yumi continues to look downcast.

* * *

Then, even before I assign partners on Tuesday, Yumi surprises me by moving her chair toward the door, asserting, "I work with Chika."

Chika looks up from the elaborate border she's drawing around her notebook page and says without interest, "What we suppose to do?"

With more patience than she has shown Chika in weeks, Yumi reiterates the instructions, and the two settle down to work. The class is studying the unreal present conditional: "If I knew her address, I'd send her a letter." ("I don't know her address, so knowing it is an unreal condition," I remind them.) The subject is quite advanced for Low Intermediate level, but several students have been asking about it.

"I know you all have goals for your future, things you want to do or be when you finish your English training," I tell them, "but let's imagine you cannot do what you thought you were going to do. Instead, let's imagine you could do or be anything else, anything in the world. If you could, what would you be? Just think for a minute."

Heba, an eye doctor back home in Kuwait, doesn't need to think. "I would be airline pilot. Fly to anywhere."

"Racing car driver, I would be." No surprise. Bing's backpack is crammed with car magazines.

Guillermo would be a television comedian, Masoud a cinnamon farmer, Jiho a chef. Fiesta, from a coastal city, reveals her dream of being a professional surfer. Mi-young, whose fiancé back in Korea sometimes troubles her by not replying to her text messages, would be happily married and have three children. Silent Won would be a singer. (Unbeknownst to me until this moment, he and Jiho have been going every weekend to karaoke night at The Hive downtown.) Chika would be an artist, but, she adds glumly, "My grandmother forbid me." Mariam would do the job she is already working toward: being a translator, perhaps at the U.N. I imagine the international incidents her capricious English might precipitate.

When Yumi's turn comes, I expect her to follow Mariam's example and declare herself dedicated to her original dream—becoming a pastor—but Yumi apologizes and shakes her head and stares into her lap. "No, nothing," she murmurs.

A troubled silence follows this remark. The students turn apprehensive glances at me. I move a little closer to Yumi.

"Nothing? Maybe a soccer coach or a sushi chef?" I blush at my lame effort to fill such a dreadful silence with inane humor. Quickly, I change the subject. "Okay then. Let's start a conditionals exercise." I instruct the partners to take turns drawing partial conditional sentences from envelopes and finishing them with the correct form. Nervously, I keep my ear tuned to Yumi's and Chika's conversation as I walk around the room. Chika's prompt, "If I were president ..." she puts back in the envelope. "I have no idea," she says, and reaches for another one.

"Yes," urges Yumi, retrieving the original prompt. "You can think of it. I help you. *'If I were president ...'* What thing you would do for your country?"

Chika shrugs. "I'm *not* president, so how I'm supposed to answer?"

"Yes, that is unreal condition," Yumi perseveres. "Condition says, 'If I *were*, but I am *not*, so I imagine *if*.'"

"Okay. *You* imagine."

"But *you* must practice."

Chika rolls her eyes. "If I am a president I will give everybody car." She tosses the prompt onto her desk and leans her chin on her palm. Yumi, catching me looking their way, turns back to Chika, anxiously.

"You cannot be a president. So, is unreal situation," Yumi presses her. "But you gave *real* situation."

"I *can* be president." Chika folds her arms across her chest. "Everybody can be a president."

"We practice If I *were*, not If I *am*."

"What's the *difference*?!" She takes another prompt from the envelope and hands it to Yumi. "*Your* turn."

By the windows, Mi-young and Won are waving their hands for help. Reluctantly, I leave my eavesdropping post and cross to the other side of the room, but as soon as I can, I hurry back. When I reach Chika and Yumi again, they're plodding through the exercise like foot-weary soldiers, and decline my offer of help.

·26·

AROUND THE FIRST OF November, there had been a premature snow. Heba, Mariam, and Guillermo stood at the window, agog. Others, from countries that could lay claim to snow, and Masoud, who had already survived three Iowa winters, beamed proprietarily. Only Chika and Yumi seemed uninspired by it. Chika looked bored. Yumi looked grim.

"We not have class tomorrow?" Chika asked hopefully.

"We *have* class," Yumi snapped at her. "Snow no matter. Even snow *this* high." She held her hand up to knee level, which—given her diminutive size—represented a more modest snowfall than she imagined.

With the cold weather has come flu. Despite teachers' pronouncements against coming to class sick, half the ESL students drag themselves to class anyway, pale and miserable and dripping with contagion, and because for many Asians audible nose blowing in public is considered disgusting, the muted sounds of learning are accompanied by a constant, irritating cacophony of sniffles. It seems to heighten the feeling that winter is wearing everyone down and sucking away the delight with which the semester began.

❊ ❊ ❊

The one delight it doesn't suck away is, surprisingly, my delight in the clumber spaniels. It's Sheryl's and Sue's first winter, and they bound through the snow (if bound is the word to describe the action of those stub-legged creatures), their drooping ears ploughing shallow trails on either side of their paw prints.

I still have the clumbers, obviously. After the first week, Doug Best e-mails to say that Rosa's father is out of danger but needs extensive rehabilitation. His whole left side is paralyzed. The family has asked Doug to stay and help with the father's mobility exercises while Rosa helps her mother look after the family business and all the younger siblings. It could be a couple of months. Kaye has offered to hire a temp to fill in while Doug is gone. Could I keep the clumbers that long?

How can I say no? Do I even want to say no? Actually, I don't. Every night as I sit at dinner, Sheryl lays her silky chin on my knee while Sue looks tactfully away from my meal, her desire evident only in the twitching of her pale, freckled eyebrows.

The neighborhood children go wild for Sheryl and Sue whenever I take them out on their leashes. The dogs submit to strenuous petting and hugging. Parents, too, come out to get a turn. Having dogs, it seems, bestows a popularity on me that I haven't lately enjoyed in my rather solitary life.

❊ ❊ ❊

And now it's mid-November. Snow has fallen and melted several times. The students from warm countries are no longer diverted by it and have begun to complain about winter just like any other Midwesterners. "It's suck!" is Guillermo's evaluation. He misses the balmy breezes of El Salvador. Masoud seems exhausted to the limit by his night job and daily commute on icy roads. I just let him sleep—better in class than on the highway. Chika is furious with Allen/Aaron, who has been too chummy with another girl at a party. Their public arguments in the hallway before and after class keep everyone abreast of the latest fluctuations in their romance.

As the weeks pass and the days grow shorter, the Koreans—Mi-young, Jiho and Won—are putting in double duty at night, doing homework and studying for the hated international TOEFL exam. Bing's lapses into daydreams of racing and luxury cars have become habitual, the doodles of Bugattis and vintage Jaguars growing thicker along the margins of his papers. Fiesta, after poking her head out of her shell earlier in the semester, now with less encouragement from her two champions, Mariam and Heba, has drawn it in again.

When I ask how meetings are going with the American conversation partners that Molly Askew-Ohashi arranged for the students, I notice tears come into Mi-young's eyes. I take her aside during the break. Is there a problem? Yes. Just when Mi-young thought she and her conversation partner, Heather, were getting along so well, Heather informed her that she didn't want to be partners anymore.

"What?" I raise an eyebrow doubtfully.

"We met at coffee shop and talk for long time," says Mi-young, holding back her tears. "More than one and half hour. Past regular fifty minutes. I thought our talking was good. She understood me. I understand her. Then—" Mi-young breaks down at this juncture. "—she said it's better not be my partner."

After Mi-young composes herself, I ask, "But what exactly did Heather say? What were her exact words? Do you remember?"

With a catch in her throat Mi-young says, "She told me, 'It's late. I better to let you go.' She fire me like John Deere." She hangs her head. "I didn't know when I should stop conversation. I was enjoying, but I know Americans are so busy people and they don't like to waste their time—"

Chika's laugh startles me. I haven't realized that she is still in the room.

"Partner just mean, 'time to go now' in polite way. No big deal."

✻ ✻ ✻

Yumi is missing class intermittently. Sometimes she leaves a message on my office voicemail: "I don't come to class today. My body has bad condition. I'm sorry. Thank you." Is it really her body condition or is it her mind condition that's bad? Yumi fails to reply to my e-mails or phone messages.

One night, after Yumi's third absence, I have a dream. In it, I get up to put on my robe, but when I reach to lift it off the hook, it isn't a robe, it's Yumi, hanging from the hook by a noose made from the robe's sash, her head inclined in a permanent bow of apology. I wake with a scream.

The day after I have this dream, Yumi attends class, participating perfunctorily. At lunch time I find her at the student center cafeteria, sitting by the windows. Her favorite lunch of mashed potatoes and beets sits uneaten on her plate while she stares into her Bible and forms its words silently on her lips. I go over and sit down.

"Yumi," I say, "I'm sorry to interrupt, but I'm kind of worried about you. Is something the matter? Can I help?"

Yumi looks up, startled. She closes her Bible. "No, no. Thank you. You are kind. Thank you. I am fine."

I shake my head. "You're not fine. You look sad. You're unhappy. Do you need to talk? Sometimes it helps to talk."

Yumi takes off her glasses and stares with a myopic gaze out the window. "It is not important," she says. Then she turns back to me. "You are kind teacher. You care your students. Thank you. But it is not important, my little problem." And she'll say no more. I sit helplessly for some seconds and then get up, with a parting reminder that if Yumi wants to talk … Yumi says, "Thank you. Maybe I come." But she isn't looking at me, and in keeping with the Japanese custom of not refusing an invitation directly, she means no.

I wonder about the upcoming Thanksgiving holiday. Does she have plans? Mariam and Heba have organized a multi-course dinner of Indonesian and Kuwaiti food for those of their classmates who have no place to go for Thanksgiving. I haven't heard that Yumi has accepted the invitation. Surely her pastor and his wife have also invited her. I ask, but she replies vaguely, "They very kind."

This is when I'm reminded of Kaye's repeated admonishments: "Jane, the University has counselors, foreign student advisors, a response team to knock on doors of depressed students. You're an ESL teacher, not a suicide prevention expert." Should I bring in the experts now? I imagine Yumi's shock and humiliation at opening her door to a suicide prevention team. There must be something *I* can do.

* * *

Her work has begun to deteriorate, and when she does attend class, she no longer takes photographs. It's the second week in November. There will be only three weeks of the semester left after Thanksgiving, and I'm afraid Yumi might fail the course. I miss the sentiment Yumi expressed for everyone during the exercise on superlatives when she declared with tears of joy in her eyes, "This is the happiest time of our life."

Chika appears oblivious to Yumi's mood change, but it troubles her other classmates, and they make numerous attempts to cheer her up. Masoud puts a free sample of Sanicorp's fennel-flavored tooth brightener in her hand. "It's new product. You can try it. Give your opinion." Mi-young, from her cell phone in class leaves voice mail messages for Yumi on the increasing number of days she doesn't show up. "Hi Yumi, I am Mi-young. I am in our classroom. Maybe you are sleeping. I hope you come soon. I miss you."

Bing scrounges together the many pens, pencils, and erasers he has borrowed from Yumi over the course of the semester and tries to get her to put them back in her pencil box, but she gently refuses. "You keep. I don't need," she says. Mariam and Heba maneuver the chairs to give Yumi a place in the little female coterie they have made with Fiesta, but Yumi, whenever she enters the classroom now, makes for the seat at the end of the row near the window. At a loss for any other way to show his concern, Guillermo escalates his tendency to call her by affectionate nicknames: Dr. Yumi, Grammar Grandma, etc.

All these kindly meant actions Yumi acknowledges politely and with a kind of muted gratitude, but her joy has disappeared and somehow this fact seems to drain away some of her classmates' former pleasure in learning as well.

❊ ❊ ❊

So on Monday I'm surprised to see Yumi, with an air of resolve, again take the empty chair next to the seat by the door where Chika usually sits. Masoud, whose seat it is customarily, almost sits on her lap when he comes in. He jumps up, apologizing. Chika arrives late and claims to have forgotten her textbook, as she so often does. In this event, she always commandeers Masoud's and looks on with him. Today, Yumi offers to share hers, but Chika pushes it away, digs deep into her backpack and extracts her own book.

Yumi draws her chair up close to Chika's and puts her finger on the paragraph in Chika's book that is being discussed. Chika pulls her book out from under Yumi's finger and turns a cold shoulder. Though constantly rebuffed, Yumi doggedly persists in these extra efforts to help. Perhaps her Bible study teacher, in the role of ecclesiastical Dear Abby, has recommended that Yumi help her enemy as a way of overcoming her antipathy toward her. Not bad advice if her enemy were willing to be helped.

·27·

ALL THE REST OF THE WEEK, Yumi is withdrawn and quiet. Everyone seems to absorb her mood. Outside, the snow has grown a gray crust. Only a jagged row of icy stumps is left of the gleaming icicles that formed earlier along the windows.

With the end of the semester drawing near, Question Man Jiho and Silent Won aren't keeping up on their homework assignments, and I suspect them of cramming for TOEFL instead. I think, Well, they probably *will* learn faster from TOEFL practice books than from anything I can offer them.

The arriving students remove their winter coats as if the pockets are weighed down by bricks. I make several more attempts to ask Yumi if she's feeling okay, if there's anything I can do to help her, but again she denies anything is wrong and, with apologies and bows, slides away. Her self-imposed isolation is now almost complete. The others treat her cautiously. Even Guillermo tosses no affectionate quips her way. She looks out of place for the first time—very elderly among fresh-faced young people, her features withered by her years. The homework she hands in is only half complete, and she forgets to put her name on it. I no longer look forward to the class; I almost dread it. I have fleeting thoughts of early retirement.

Then, on Wednesday, the day before the four-day Thanksgiving break, Yumi surprises everyone by arriving with a container of homemade sushi and bustles about as of old, distributing the goods. The class mood rises perceptibly.

"It's just vegetable," she assures Guillermo and Heba, who once expressed their astonishment that anyone would willingly eat raw fish.

"Thank you!" says Jiho. "I don't have time for eaten breakfast today!"

Yumi puts napkins down for everyone and after bowing and ceremoniously giving me mine ("Extra pieces, because teacher!"), she next offers sushi to Chika, who has just slid into her chair, ten minutes late. Chika curls her lip. She doesn't like sushi, she says.

"Not like sushi!" exclaims Mi-young. "Japanese who not likes sushi? Impossible!"

"So you're not Japanese?" jokes Guillermo.

Chika doesn't eat breakfast; she's on a diet, she asserts.

It's hard to know if she's deliberately being rude to Yumi just when Yumi seems to be pulling herself out of her slump, or if she is simply oblivious. Yumi's smile goes dead on her face, and she passes the rest of the sushi around without comment.

Despite this latest snub, Yumi once again claims Chika as her partner. Brusquely, she gestures for Chika to bring her chair closer, a command Chika pretends not to notice until Yumi gets up and pushes her own chair over. Chika crosses her arms over her chest.

A few seconds later, I hear Chika's loud mocking laugh. Glancing back from across the room, I see something like desolation, or perhaps fear, on Yumi's face.

Chika says something to her. Yumi replies. They exchange a few more words, and then, seeming to become as small as possible, Yumi draws into herself. In contrast to Chika's defiant upturned chin, cocked head, and impatient, jiggling foot, Yumi's chin is tucked in almost to her clavicle, her knees locked together and her arms wrapped around her chest as if she is encased in an invisible strait-jacket.

"All right," I call out suddenly, causing a few students to jump. "Let's trade partners now."

It takes some minutes before Yumi uncurls, even with her new partner Mi-young, who takes Chika's vacated chair and tentatively draws Yumi back into the practice exercise. I keep a close watch on them, but Yumi's face is unreadable.

* * *

Meddling be damned. Suicide prevention team move over. Let Kaye tell me off; I've waited long enough to act.

Gathering courage, I stop Yumi as the students are filing out of class and rather solemnly ask her to come to my office. I mean business. She looks fearful. We walk to Addams Hall in silence.

I invite her in, but she advances only a single step just inside the open door next to the bookcase and glances over at Molly's side of the room.

"My office mate is at lunch now," I assure her and close the door.

Yumi has started to breathe raspily, and I see that she is trying to control tears.

I put my hand on her arm. "What's the matter, Yumi? I know something's wrong. You must tell me."

She won't come when I try to lead her to the student chair but accepts a tissue and lifts her glasses to mop her eyes.

"Did something upset you?" I ask foolishly. Yumi shakes her head, her face averted. "Is it something about your class work?"

"Thank you, Teacher, I'm sorry," she says in a small, quavering voice, and bows several times.

"How can I help you?"

Blinking away her tears with an attempt to smile, Yumi says again, "I'm sorry. Nothing. Thank you. I'm sorry."

She continues to stand by the bookcase, pressing the tissue against her eyes. I wonder if I should go away and leave her alone. Maybe

141

she wants to cry privately. But she might want comfort and be too overcome or ashamed to say so. How can I know?

"Please, Yumi," I say, "sit down and stay as long as you want." This time Yumi lets me lead her to the chair. For a minute or so, we sit together in silence except for Yumi's involuntary gasping sobs. Intermittently, I pat her on the arm. Then Yumi gets up to go.

"Thank you, Teacher. I'm sorry," she says.

"You don't have to leave yet. You're welcome to stay longer."

Was it Chika's rebuffs when Yumi tried to make amends for the picture snatching incident? I should have diverted Yumi from such a fruitless mission. No one could placate that spoiled brat. Or maybe it was Yumi's seventy-eight percent on the conditionals quiz? What was I thinking to introduce such an advanced topic? When Yumi saw that she had scored below ninety for the first time, she pondered the number bleakly without searching to correct her wrong answers, and then put the quiz out of sight under her notebook. Everyone else seemed a bit depressed by the quiz, too. I clearly overestimated the class's proficiency, or I hadn't adequately prepared them for the quiz. What a mess I've made of things.

"Yumi, I'm worried. You seem to be losing your enthusiasm for your studies—" At this, Yumi drops her head. "You're an excellent student, an extremely intelligent person," I hasten to add. "That's why I'm worried." No reply. I talk on nervously. "I'm only concerned that something is bothering you. I don't mean to pry into your private feelings—" Jane, Jane, McBee has counselors ... "—maybe it would be useful—if you need someone to talk to—"

"I can not ..." Yumi interrupts in a low voice.

"You cannot *what?*" I lean forward to catch the murmured words. But Yumi presses her lips closed then, as if locking them against further confession. She rises from her chair suddenly and bows once, about to make her escape.

"Wait, Yumi. Is there anything I can do? If I accidentally did something to hurt your feelings, I—"

Yumi's face screws up, like a child's before it breaks into a wail, but she only presses her lips tighter, intensifying the grimace, and shakes her head. She starts for the door. Then she stops, seems to reconsider, and turns back.

"No. No," she says. "Teacher Jane, you never hurt my feelings. Thank you. I'm sorry." Avoiding my eyes she stares at my family photo on the desk. She lowers herself into the chair, and in a voice choked with anguish says, "I cannot love her. No matter I play—" She corrects herself. "—No matter how much I praying."

"Love ... who?" But of course I know.

Yumi's hand worries the small cross that hangs at the throat of her open coat. "I praying and praying," she says, "but I do not love her."

"Yumi." I take her other hand, cold and stiff, in mine. "Chika is hard to love right now at this time of her life." Yumi doesn't reply. "Why should you expect yourself to love her? I'm not so happy with her at the moment either."

Still staring at the photo she says, "You love her, Teacher, in your heart. But I do not."

I clutch the unresponsive hand. "Yumi, Chika has many people in her life who love her. She'll be fine without your love, too." Yumi seems to wince at this and hangs her head.

Why did I tiptoe around Chika, ignoring her conspicuous smirks and snorts and sighs and curled lips, her sleeping in class and coming in late? What if I had extracted a public apology from Chika for that "Who *cares!*" remark? If I had chastised her before she flounced out of the classroom, would Yumi have been able to love her then, out of sympathy?

"We can't always love everybody!" I entreat her.

"I must," Yumi replies. "I must love enemy, love neighbor, turn cheek. But I can't do. I must, but I can't forgive my whole life. I can't forgive. That's my fault. I am not good Christian." She slides her hand from mine and stands up. "I'm sorry. Thank you. I'm sorry." Clutching the tissue, with head bowed, she leaves my office.

Should I go after her? She has only twenty minutes to get lunch and pull herself together before her afternoon classes—if she even intends to show up for class. I let her go.

I sit at my desk wondering how I ever imagined that teaching was my calling. Wondering how to convince a person that her entire worth as a human being does not ride on following Biblical exhortations to the letter.

·28·

THAT AFTERNOON, I take the campus bus to the bottom of the hill, but walk the rest of the way home despite the ice patches skulking on the snow-packed sidewalks. It's hard to enjoy winter as I once did, always being nagged these days by the fear, at sixty-two, of falling and incurring some disabling injury that will defy treatment and define the rest of my life.

I have to concentrate on the ice and not let my thoughts wander to Yumi's impossible demand on herself and my own backfired attempt at reassurance. "Chika will be fine without your love, too." Stupid thing to say. Yumi will take that sentence in and brood over my opinion of her.

For most of the way home I walk on the snow-encrusted strip of grass between sidewalk and street, where the footing isn't so slick. When my little bungalow is at last in sight, I stop to rest. With the crunch of snow no longer in my ears, I notice that the air is filled with the cries of raucous birds.

Five crows, enormous and omen-like, stand in the middle of the street on territory once claimed by the rabbit. The birds all face in different directions as if in a snit and pointedly ignoring each other. As I approach, they rise up on their legs, one by one in slow motion, spread their wings wide and flap up into the branches of a tall sycamore tree, knocking patches of snow to the ground. Masses of crows are perched in the very top of the tree, forming a great black umbrella of cawing birds. Their droppings dapple the snow. I move hurriedly out from under the line of fire.

I make my way down the rest of the block and step with relief onto the solid concrete of my own sidewalk. The birds scared me a little, even though I've seen this mobbing of crows every season and know that nothing ever comes of it. They scream insults and dirty the ground for a day or two and then fly away. But today my little bit of fear fills me with dismay. Somehow, there are things I never seem to learn, no matter how many times I experience them. I often tell my students that mistakes teach us useful lessons. But have I learned from my own mistakes? When I retire, will I leave the profession feeling I never quite got beyond the novice stage?

I've failed to motivate Chika. Yumi has lost all her lovely zest for learning and her self-confidence while in my class. And the other students—how much, after all, have they progressed in these three months? And then there's Donna, whom I was supposed to have mentored. She has, if anything, become a worse teacher than when she started.

* * *

That night, I put the dogs in the basement, wander into the living room, turn off the lights, and draw back the curtains to look at the snow. The whiteness outside and the yellow cone of the single street light at the end of the cul de sac illuminate the dark room. It's snowing again. I step onto my porch and stand for a while in the sharp, crisp air watching the snow swirl around the street light. A freight train on the overpass two blocks away squeals to a stop with the sound of a hundred string instruments tuning up. Its cessation accentuates the deep silence of the falling snow.

Now the snow is coming down heavily and at such a slant that it seems to be pouring from the street light. In the front yard, an indistinct dark form casts a stunted shadow. A lingering crow? Not the right shape. Did it move just then?

I stare hard at it for a minute or two. I could swear it moved slightly. But, no, after another minute, I conclude I'm mistaken and go back inside. Then, out of the corner of my eye, I catch the movement through the window again. The object leaps straight into the air. It's the rabbit.

It sits still for long intervals on the shadowy white lawn, and then turns a little in one direction and a little in another before suddenly leaping and landing several feet away from where it started, to face in a third direction. I've seen rabbits leap over each other while courting or fighting, but do they ever leap alone? I watch it for some time. And then I realize what I'm seeing. The rabbit is trying to leap over its own shadow, but its shadow is always one jump ahead.

I can't bear to watch, and turn from the window. Will that poor bunny keep it up all night, hour after hour puzzled and frustrated by these futile attempts to mate or engage an inexplicably elusive rival? But surely a rabbit can smell the difference between a shadow and a creature of its own kind.

Maybe it's leaping only for fun, just because it feels frolicsome on a snowy night. It's quite possible to enjoy a solo frolic. If not for scaring the rabbit away, I wouldn't mind going out there and frolicking in the snow myself, just to cheer up. It's something my whimsical, spontaneous mother might have done. She would have been in her eighties now if cancer hadn't carried her off.

I find myself thinking of Yumi and wondering if Yumi misses her mother, too, assuming she's not still alive. I wonder what sad things happened to Yumi's mother to make Yumi say, wistfully looking at my family photo, "Your mother was so happy." And I also wonder why Yumi can't bring herself to forgive Chika. Of course Chika is the only student in class who is disrespectful in addition to being unmotivated. How can I convince Yumi that it's possible to break the "Gordon Lure" once in a while and still be a person worthy of love herself?

That night I lie in bed thinking about Yumi and about the rabbit. Only weeks ago I entertained the image of my neighbor's beagle slaughtering the greedy marauder, and I sadistically relished the thought of cayenne pepper burning the rabbit's tongue. But ever since drawing the animal's portrait, I've been inclined to protect it. Does your enemy appear different to you when you take it on as a project?

That may have been Yumi's failed strategy: Teach Unreal Conditionals to Thine Enemy. Convey Modal Auxiliaries Unto Others. If Chika had been willing to be taught or done unto, the strategy might have worked. Now Yumi hates Chika all the more; yet, to consider herself worthy of God's love, she has to love her, and for Yumi to love her, Chika has to accept her attempts to help, but the more Yumi tries to give her help, the more Chika rejects it.

These thoughts begin to loop through my brain in that annoying way that puts you beyond sleep. I open my bedside soporific, *The Country of the Pointed Firs*, and read a chapter of Sarah Orne Jewett's slow, elegant, quieting prose. At last I drift off.

✳ ✳ ✳

The next morning, on Thanksgiving Day, I sit bolt upright in bed with something to be thankful for—the solution to Yumi's dilemma, fully formed. It has come to me in a flash out of a half-dreaming state. A plan to give Yumi her happiness back. It seems to me it can't fail. The only problem is I'll have to violate FERPA.

✳ ✳ ✳

On Monday after the holiday, I dress for work, considering the ways and means of executing my idea, gauging its moral and legal considerations and its chance of success. None of my colleagues would approve. It's the kind of unprofessional busy-bodying that I myself would firmly veto if someone else proposed it. The plan is devious, manipulative and unethical.

But I think of Yumi's tears spilling and streaming down like little rivulets into the deep arroyos of her worn, desolate face as she sat in my office holding back sobs. Yumi's very life might depend on Chika's good behavior. Am I overdramatizing the situation? No. Surely it's a crisis calling for bold and immediate action.

I hesitate to run my idea by Molly, making her a conspirator, and I certainly can't run it by Kaye, who would cite the FERPA regulations and warn me not to even think about it. For breaking FERPA rules you can be fired, and the program—even the University—can be sued ... I stop to wonder at myself. I can appreciate the purpose of rules and regulations, yet in this case wouldn't it be reprehensible to fear legalities and fail to act when I see a way to resurrect Yumi's joy? Yes. It would. It could easily backfire, of course, and I have ceased being a screw-the-establishment risk-taker, but I can't get those words out of my mind: *Whole my life was bad time ... I was rough child ... Your mother was so happy, I think,* and that dream—Yumi with a noose around her neck, her head bent in a permanent bow of apology.

That morning I put the plan in motion. Just as Chika is running off to her boyfriend at the end of Low Intermediate Grammar/Writing, I stop her and request that she come to my office.

"Why?" Chika demands.

"I just want to go over a few things with you."

Her eyes narrow. "I must tell *Ponyo* movie again?"

"No."

"How long it takes?"

"Not long."

"I hand in my homework."

"I know you did. It's nothing to do with that."

Chika considers for a moment. She shrugs. "Okay. Just I have to buy my lunch. Then I come."

Chika's afternoon classes start at 1:00, and by 12:30 she hasn't shown up. I'm afraid she won't turn up at all. I've banished Molly by mentioning that I am to have a rather delicate conference with a student. Now I sit in my office with time to obsess over whether this is such a good idea. FERPA rules dance in my head. And I can't keep Molly away indefinitely. She might need to come and pick up her class binders. Maybe it's for the best. If Molly comes back before Chika gets here, I will just forget the idea, relieve myself of the worry that I'm violating federal regulations and—

Chika arrives at 12:35 without apology and sits down uninvited in my student chair. She doesn't take off her coat. Immediately she begins to parse her split ends, keeping her eyelids at half-mast to display her imperviousness to any reprimand I might want to inflict on her.

"Chika," I begin after she's gotten as settled as she's likely to get. "I called you in to ask you for a special favor, but it has to be an absolute secret."

Her half-mast lids fly up. She drops her damaged tresses. "What secret?"

I get up and make a show of closing the door. I turn and look at her somberly. "Maybe you've noticed lately that Yumi is not happy?"

Chika slumps back in her chair. "She's got bad mood." *So what.*

"I think she's very discouraged about her English."

Chika sniffs. "Her English is better more than me."

"Yes, but Yumi is an older woman, and she's old-fashioned. She doesn't think she's progressing as fast as she should."

Chika looks skeptical. "She get A every time."

"Not anymore." I'm in it now. I've just committed my first FERPA violation by disclosing Yumi's academic information. I take a breath. Might as well go the whole hog. "I'm worried about Yumi, I'm afraid she's becoming seriously depressed." Private personal information. Check.

Chika blinks and sits up a little.

I pull my chair closer and say, confidingly, "I have an idea about how to get her out of her depression, and I'm asking you to help me."

"Me?" The truculent scowl returns to Chika's face. "Sometimes Yumi act mean to me. She don't give me picture and thing like that."

"Yes, I know. But in the beginning she wasn't mean to you. Remember? I think she's mean to you now because she feels bad about herself." Chika seems to consider this. I push my advantage. "Haven't you ever done that, when you felt sad or worried about something, been mean to other people? I've done it myself, haven't you?"

"Sometime," she concedes.

"I've thought of a way to make Yumi feel better about herself, and I wonder if you would mind helping me—" Chika's brow furrows. *Me?* "—I think it would be more impressive coming from you," I hurry to say, "because you're Japanese, too, and maybe you can understand her situation better than her other classmates can." I lean toward her and say in a low voice, "It has to be a secret because Yumi might feel ashamed if she knows we're trying to help her."

I have her attention now. "So here's my idea." I stop a moment for dramatic effect, and cock my head as if to listen for imaginary eavesdroppers outside the door. Chika glances at the door, too. "I want you to start asking Yumi questions about English."

Chika frowns. "What questions?"

"Anything. If we're studying something in our book, even if you know the answer, ask her about it. Ask *Why* questions, like '*Why is it this way?*' or *When* questions—'*When do we use this?*' or '*How do we make it?*'—"

"I ask Yes/No question, too? '*Do you ...?*' '*Do I ...?*' '*Is it?*' Like that?"

"Yes/No questions, too. Any questions about the grammar or vocabulary. But," I shake my finger for emphasis, "you have to be careful! Don't suddenly ask too *many* questions. Be like an actor—as if you're in a movie. You have to play the role of someone who needs help, you have to act a little shy about it, so she will believe that you want her help."

"Like Fiesta."

"Yes, like Fiesta." If Fiesta ever *asked* questions.

"Why you want me to ask questions?"

"Can't you guess?"

"Make Yumi feel like she's know a lot of thing? Like expert?"

"Exactly. You know a lot about American idioms. Isn't it fun to explain them to people who don't know? It feels good to be an expert, doesn't it?" Chika nods. "In the same way, Yumi will feel good, too."

"When I should ask questions?"

"Any time. In class, walking to class, at lunch in the student center. But remember, be an actor. Play the role *believably*. You have to start slowly. It can't seem fake. Do you understand what I mean?"

"Just one day I ask one question—'Yumi, why my #3 answer is wrong?' Next day other question like I just remember it?"

"Perfect. That's it. And don't tell anyone. Yumi must not suspect."

A smile breaks across Chika's face. It's quite startling to see it. She looks charming. She flicks her orange bangs out of her eyes and crosses her legs in a parody of a movie star.

"Piece of cake," she says.

·29·

'M SITTING BY MY fireplace fretting, the clumbers stretched out beside me. A glowing cinder jumps out and lands close to the wool rug. I kick it back into the fire with the toe of my slipper. Chika might easily tell one of the other students about my plan and then they'll all start trying to help, and Yumi will catch on and feel embarrassed, and things will get worse for her. Or Chika might tell students in other classes, and everyone will know, and Kaye might even get wind of it.

The whole program could get sued over my breach of University rules. Of course Yumi herself wouldn't dream of suing anyone for any reason, but I remember the brouhaha at McBee when a student failed a test and accused the teacher of plagiarism because parts of the test were excerpted from a textbook without citation. The teacher hadn't been trying to claim authorship of the excerpts, but he hadn't cited them properly and the student had a grudge.

Chika has a grudge. She blames the McBee ESL Program, Kaye Bibber, and all her teachers for not promoting her. It's our fault that she isn't learning fast enough. And I just remembered that Chika knows about FERPA because I, like a fool, explained it to her.

More likely, though, the worst that will happen is Chika will decide she can't be bothered to do anything for Yumi, and Yumi will keep hating her and hating herself for hating her.

I stare into the lively, cheerful flames and consider this gloomy

153

possibility. Too bad the New Testament doesn't get more specific: Here is how to love thine enemy who pusheth thy buttons. What are Yumi's buttons? She was so happy at first, like a little bumble bee in the sunshine, just buzzing around the class and dropping golden motivation pollen on everybody's heads. Nothing bothered her then, not even Chika.

❋ ❋ ❋

Chika slouches into class ten minutes late as usual the next day, the first of December, as sullen and disengaged as always, and takes the only remaining seat, between Bing and the door. With forced composure, I pass out the pair work exercise instructions as my hopes for my plan fade. Chika has missed my preliminary explanation of how the synonyms *must* and *have to* become opposites in the negative—*must not, don't have to.*

"Why?" queries Masoud, throwing his hands up in despair.

"Interesting English," elucidates Guillermo.

The distinction between *must not* and *don't have to* was taught in Chika's class last semester, but I would bet my dwindling retirement investments that Chika didn't pay attention then, just as she isn't paying attention now. Is there any point in pairing Yumi with Chika today as I've planned? Is there the slightest chance that Chika took my secret assignment to heart after leaving my office?

Today she has turned herself into a veritable boredom machine, all functions set on high: one leg in jiggle mode, her left hand engaged in quality control on damaged hair strands, her right hand toggling a pencil up and down between her thumb and forefinger. Across the room, Yumi sits with shoulders bowed and hands resting limp on her lap. Her once busy pen lies across her open book as if felled.

I have to make up my mind quickly. The students are looking to me for their pair assignments. Well, if it's not going to happen, I might as well find out now.

"Masoud and Jiho," I announce, "Mi-young and Bing, Won and Guillermo, Mariam, Heba and Fiesta, and ... Yumi and Chika."

In the general picking up of books, pencil cases and notebooks, the risings and shiftings of places, Yumi's immobility and Chika's inertia seem painfully conspicuous. I hold my breath.

It's Chika who finally complies, rising and dragging her feet over to the place next to Yumi with the resigned sigh of one being forced to give up a fifth row center theatre seat.

"Okay, everybody," I say brightly. "Talk about necessary and unnecessary things that happen in fall and in winter in Zenith, and be careful about your verb tenses. For example," I add, pointing to the sentence on the blackboard, "now, in winter we *have to* (or *must*) wear heavy coats and gloves, but in fall we *didn't have to*."

For the next ten minutes, I'm occupied with various legalistic disputes such as Won's insistence that the use of *have to* is reasonable in the sentence, "Leaves don't have to fall from trees in winter" ("because they already fall"), and some misunderstandings about the concept "lack of necessity" as in Bing's assertion (technically true) that "in winter I don't have to have barefoot outside."

Just as I'm edging closer to monitor the Chika/Yumi duo, which appears from a distance to be at a standstill, I have to attend to the Mariam/Heba/Fiesta trio, whose quiet exchanges have suddenly turned to emotional cries and pleas for my intervention.

"What's happening?" I inquire.

Fiesta's face is red and Heba is gesticulating with her heavily ringed hands. "Jane!" she commands. "Tell her we don't mean offending her. Only we are—"

"She's think we are offend her," breaks in Mariam, "but we're not mean offend but just we—"

"We want to know—"

"We want to know what it's feel like. Because we must not drink it. So we never drink it."

"Drink … ?" I look from their earnest, anxious faces to Fiesta's flushed one.

"Alcohol," the Muslim women say in unison.

"We are just …" Mariam searches for the word.

"Curious?" I suggest.

"Yes! Yes!" That is the word that's eluded them.

Fiesta's mouth hangs open. It seems to me that she also is trying to come up with a word. I turn to Fiesta. "Do you understand the reason they're asking?"

Fiesta nods vehemently and half rises from her seat. With what seems like a great effort, she releases the words.

"I'm not offend!" she protests. "Only I cannot explain …"

"Explain what it feels like to drink alcohol?" Fiesta nods eagerly.

"Jane," Mariam asks rather breathlessly, "you have ever drunken alcohol?"

"Yes, I have. I used to drink alcohol when I was younger. And now sometimes I have a glass of wine in the evening."

"How it feels?"

All three women raise expectant faces.

I think for a moment, seeing myself, a young woman in a smoky bar dancing uninhibitedly to a Motown beat, flirting outrageously with strangers, contemplating through the haze of smoke the sweetness and perfection of all the people raising glasses around me.

"Well," I say, "when I drank alcohol, I loved *everybody!*"

In one startling movement, Fiesta leaps from her chair and clutches my arm.

"Teacher *understands!*" she shouts, and for the first time since being on the winning side in the September soccer match, she grins —as the saying goes—from ear to ear.

This surprising little drama has distracted me from my primary preoccupation, and after I leave the trio discussing the necessity or lack thereof of abstaining from alcohol, I move quietly to within listening distance behind the desk chairs of Chika and Yumi.

Yumi is saying, "—because *had to* is past form to *must*."

"Not *did must*?" asks Chika.

"No. *Did must* is wrong," Yumi replies brusquely.

"So *didn't have to* means ...?"

"Was not necessary."

"And *must not* mean 'not necessary' too?"

"No. *Must not* meaning is 'prohibited, not allow.'"

Chika peers down at the book open to the summary of prohibition and necessity modals. "So is right I can say, 'In fall I had to take Low Intermediate level class again, but anyway I did not have to come back Japan'?"

Yumi considers this. After a moment she says, "Yes. It's right."

I've been standing behind them all the while and now accidentally release an audible breath. Chika turns slightly and looks up at me with a deadpan expression. I return her look with a hint of a smile. Chika has come to class today well-rehearsed in the role of Chika.

·30·

THE NEXT DAY, Chika is on time for a change, a little early in fact, and as soon as she comes in the door, she heads straight for Yumi, who, in an odd reflex when she sees Chika descending on her, takes off her glasses.

I cringe. Chika is going to overdo it. Oh dear. I sidle nearer and strain to hear the two, over the sounds of other students entering and settling into their seats.

Having flounced up to Yumi, Chika pulls out her textbook, opens it to a bookmarked page, and thrusts it at her. "Your way is not correct," she asserts. "Yesterday you said, 'for compare *bored* must have *more*, but here is Rule 1—" she slaps the open book on Yumi's desktop. "—says 'one syllable adjective, add *-er*.' 'Bored' have one syllable, so *boreder* is correct. I'm right."

Yumi's brow knits and she blinks several times, unsmiling, before she returns her large glasses to her face and peers through them at Rule #1 for the formation of comparatives. Making no eye contact with Chika, she quotes: "'Most short adjectives—not all—add *-er*.'" She draws a finger down the page to a footnote. "*Bored* is exception."

Chika reads the exceptions aloud to herself: *tired, bored, fun*. "Oh," she says sulkily and sits down in the empty desk next to Yumi. "I'm wrong."

For a moment Yumi does nothing. Then she turns toward Chika, though not quite looking at her, and says, "You did read textbook, that's good for you, but you must *carefully* read."

I suck in a breath through clenched teeth. Now openly watching, I hold the breath and wait.

Chika makes a petulant *moue* and shrugs. She says, "You are more better reader than me, so it's easy. But for me it's not."

My mouth drops. I lean in closer, but neither of the two notices. Yumi darts a glance Chika's way. Then she gently closes Chika's textbook, lifts it from her own desktop and just as gently puts it in Chika's hands.

By now all the students have arrived. I pull myself away and start class.

What has just taken place? Is it just a happy, accidental confluence of Chika's gracelessness and arrogance? Or has Chika set out deliberately to make Yumi a sincere compliment disguised as a backhanded one? Is she capable of such subtlety?

I call her to my office for a report. Chika settles into the student chair and starts in outlining her next steps.

"I must get grade on test almost good as Yumi but not better." She has also involved her boyfriend Allen in the ruse. "Because Aaron is American, he don't know what is adjective clause, so I told him we ask Yumi." She laughs. "Yumi explained to us and he say 'I get it.' But after, he tell me, 'I still don't get it.' *He* still don't understand adjective clause, but *I* know now because Yumi explained."

My heart takes an extra beat. "Your boyfriend knows about this plan?"

"No way!" Chika scoffs. "Aaron would be screw up because he can't tell lie with being comfortable."

I relax. "Chika, you're doing a wonderful job. So you're going to keep going?"

"I must keep going. If I stop to do it, she get more depression."

"And if you stop doing it, she might get worried about *your* English progress."

Chika raises one side of her mouth skeptically. "No. She doesn't care me."

❖ ❖ ❖

On Thursday, Masoud produces his latest language discoveries: "Uh oh," "uh huh," "huh!" and "huh?" His Vietnamese co-worker Truong explained each one to him as they passed toothpaste tubes down the quality control line together.

"'Uh oh' mean trouble happen, 'uh huh' is yes, 'uh uh' is no, 'huh!' mean it's interesting, and 'huh?' mean *What* you say?" Masoud so admires the simplicity and precision of these expressions that I decide not to inform him that in certain formal contexts, uh huh, uh uh and huh? are considered somewhat impolite.

It's December already, with two weeks of the semester to go. I haven't paired Yumi and Chika for several days, so I decide it might not look too contrived if I have them peer review each other's personal essays reflecting on their semester of English study.

Chika's essay, as usual, is short. She claims to have nothing interesting to say. "Everything here except study English is good," she writes. "I hate to study hardly."

Yumi points out that "hardly" is not an adverb form of "hard."

"Yes," Chika insists. "Just you add –*ly* to make adverb, like 'quick, quickly'." She flips through the textbook to the page on adverbs of manner and points at the rule.

Yumi points at the asterisked footnote explaining "hardly" as a quantifier meaning "scarcely." "Read whole rules!" she admonishes.

A few minutes later, from Yumi's and Chika's corner comes a loud "Ha!" I slide over.

"Read *whole rules!*" Chika gloats, holding open the textbook.

Yumi has written, "At airport I walked lonely to my gate."

"Exceptions!" exclaims Chika. "'Lonely' is adjective not adverb. Like 'friendly.' You are friendly. Not you *walk* friendly." She notices me hovering. "Right?"

When has she started to pay attention? When did she learn the difference between an adjective and an adverb?

Yumi concedes the point. She learned the exceptions weeks before, but in her malaise has forgotten them. From her voluminous pencil case she takes out a highlighter pen and draws pink circles around the exceptions: lonely, friendly, lovely. Chika holds out a hand for Yumi's highlighter, and Yumi watches as she draws a pink circle in her own book around the footnoted word "hardly."

"One mistake for you, one mistake for me," says Chika.

Yumi gazes down for some seconds at the word "hardly." "You are a smart girl," she says. Chika hands back the highlighter pen, but Yumi waves it away. "You can keep."

* * *

A competition has apparently arisen between them, almost a friendly rivalry. Yumi is studying again, and Chika appears to be studying for the first time. Even their other teacher notices it. "Yumi seems to be coming out of her funk," comments Molly Askew-Ohashi on Friday. "I guess it was just mid-semester blues. Chika isn't doing so badly either, miracle of miracles!"

I call Chika in for a third consultation.

"What do you think," I ask. "Is it working?"

Chika nods complacently.

"I have strategy." The strategy is to comb the textbook for typical grammatical pitfalls and deliberately fall into them. "I think Yumi like to explain those tricky part. And now I know, too." Smugly, she adds, "She has a little depression now."

"Less, you mean? *Only* a little?"

Chika thinks for a moment. "'Little,' 'only a little,' 'a little.' That's tricky." She rummages through her backpack and pulls out a notepad filled with writing. At the top of a new page she adds "little," "only a little," "a little."

"It's in Chapter Four."

"Oh yeah." Chapter 4, Chika writes.

* * *

"Why I can say 'I don't like to study,' but I cannot say 'I dislike to study'? Why it's wrong? They are same!"

Chika directs this protest at Yumi, but so loudly that the whole class answers automatically: "Interesting English!"

"There is no reason," Yumi explains, irritably. "Just you have to remember."

"But I can say," Chika persists, "'I stopped smoking' and 'I stopped to smoke.' They are same."

"Yes, you can say, but they are not same meaning."

"Same!"

"Different."

Chika's hand flies in the air and I come over inquiringly as if I've not been eavesdropping.

"Stop smoking and stop to smoke are same, right?"

"Actually—"

Chika takes a cigarette pack from her pocket, pulls out a cigarette and pretends to throw it away. "I stop smoking," she declares. "I stop to smoke."

Suddenly Yumi, without a word, takes up Chika's cigarette pack, rises from her chair and comes to the front of the room. She removes a cigarette and holds it to her mouth. The whole class watches, astonished. Then Yumi shakes her head vigorously and throws the cigarette onto the table. "I stop smoking," she says.

Next, still holding the pack, Yumi, on her short bow legs, saunters around the room for a few seconds and then halts. She pulls out a second cigarette and pantomimes lighting up and taking a puff. "I stop to smoke," she says.

Guillermo snatches off his backward facing cap and throws it in the air.

"Bravo!" he shouts over the applause.

And everybody understands that Yumi is with us again.

Chika twitches a barely detectable smile at me.

·31·

'M COMING BACK through the main office feeling, well, triumphant. Yes, triumphant. I've pulled Yumi out of her funk and simultaneously accomplished what no other teacher has come close to. I've motivated Chika.

As I walk toward my office, Sangkyun, a tall, gentle-spoken Korean boy in Donna's class, stops me to ask if there's a map of campus town and how he can find the business whose owner he has chosen to interview for Donna's Communication Skills assignment. The boy's accent is very slight. There is no confusion of r's and l's or of p's and f's or any other typical Koreanisms. In fact, I realize that he is one of the most fluent, clear-spoken students in Intermediate level—the last one to need special help with pronunciation.

It occurs to me that he is the only Korean in Donna's classes.

In my office I mull this over. If Sangkyun is the only Korean in Donna's classes, and he doesn't need pronunciation help, why is Donna so eager to learn about the English pronunciation problems of Koreans? A comment of Donna's comes to mind from several weeks earlier when she asked for pronunciation help with Arabic speakers. "And what about Indian speakers?" she said. "What do *they* need?"

There are no Indian speakers in McBee ESL. I had mentioned this to her, but she was "just curious," and my "expertise" in pronunciation was so "impressive," that she "couldn't get enough of it."

164

And now it starts to come together. The Fridays off—not just laziness or self-indulgence, but—I go to my computer and Google the search terms *Donna Bittner* and *pronunciation*. There are several Donna Bittners—an insurance agent in Indianapolis, a winning women's basketball coach at a college in Wisconsin ... I have to scroll to the fifth page of Donna Bittner references before I find what I'm looking for.

It's a small blurb under Employee Benefits in the personnel section of the corporate website of Worldwide InfoTech Services, located in Des Moines, Iowa. The section announces company-sponsored, on-the-job accent reduction classes for its non-native employees. *Instructor: D. Renee Bittner, MA, certified ESL Instructor and Pronunciation Specialist. Classes held Fridays 9:00-4:00 every hour on the hour. Eligible employees must be recommended for classes and registered by their unit manager or immediate supervisor.*

Bingo.

Not only has Donna been working a second job on days when McBee University is paying her to teach, but clearly the only thing she knows about teaching pronunciation is the bits and pieces she has picked from my brain.

❖ ❖ ❖

On my home computer I scan the Worldwide InfoTech Services employee directory and count the number of non-native names. It's a large company with seven Koreans, eleven Chinese, fifteen Indians, and ten other miscellaneous nationalities.

I'm hopeless at imitating Chinese and Korean accents, even though I've been teaching these students for twenty-four years. But I can do something that, to Westerners unfamiliar with Indian-English dialects, can pass for an Indian accent. I just curl my tongue back on *t*'s and *d*'s, turn *th*'s into *t*'s, *w*'s to *v*'s and vice versa, trill the *r*'s, throw in some Britishisms and unexpected syllable stress, use

165

impeccable grammar and vocabulary that is highly precise but a bit too formal in register. As Bing would say, piece of a cake.

"Vedy obedient dogs," I say to Sheryl and Sue, who are standing by with heads cocked, waiting out my rehearsal. "Have no doubt. I will trow your ball for you momentarily. Do not vorry." I write my script and practice the accent until I'm satisfied.

❖ ❖ ❖

On Monday morning when Molly is out of the office, I take a deep breath, picture myself in a sari, and make the call to the personnel office of Worldwide InfoTech Services.

"Good afternoon, Madam. I am inquiring about the accent reduction classes of our company on Fridays. I tink this class would be of benefit to me. How vould I go about participating?"

"Your immediate supervisor has to send a request for you," replies the personnel officer. "The supervisor can choose a time slot that's most convenient for the employee to be away from the department. The request form is on the personnel website."

"I see, tank you. Excuse me, who, might I ask, teaches these classes?"

"The instructor's name is Renee Bittner."

"Renee? I tought I heard someone to remark that her given name is Donna?"

"No … Oh … Yes, it *is* Donna, but she goes by Renee."

"And, excuse me, but she is an experienced teacher? She's a native American?"

"A native speaker? Yes. She has a master's degree in ESL with special training in accent reduction. She's a very enthusiastic and friendly gal. I think you'll like her."

"Tank you wedy much."

"Actually the classes are all full at the moment, but tell me your name and your supervisor, and I'll—"

"I am sorry, Madame, I must ring you back. I am summoned to a meeting. Tank you. I will ring you back." I hang up, damp in the armpits.

I sit for a while feeling quite the Nancy Drew Girl Detective just before her father, Carson Drew the Famous Criminal Lawyer, arrives to commend her on a job well done. Then I get up and go to tell Kaye Bibber the news.

Kaye looks grave after she hears me out. She has put aside another upsetting memo from the Dean, asking for budget figures. He doesn't have to tell her what he wants them for. She knows he's trying to make a case for the imagined economic benefits of *GET IN!*

She goes to her personnel files and pulls out Donna's folder to find the phone number of the southern California university where Donna has recently gotten her master's degree in Linguistics with a specialty in Teaching English as a Second Language. She punches in the number.

"I'm thinking of giving Donna Bittner a pronunciation class next semester," Kaye tells the ESL Coordinator, "and I wonder how intensive her phonology and phonetics coursework was when she was a graduate student in Linguistics."

There's a pause. Kaye frowns. "What do you mean?" Another pause. Kaye's eyebrows rise. "She accepted our offer last May, and she's teaching here now. She's been here since August." I scoot my chair in closer. "Lincoln, Nebraska? ... But what's she doing there? ... Really? Are you sure?"

I sit forward on the edge of my chair. "But we *did* contact her," Kaye protests. "I sent her an acceptance letter."

This back and forth goes on for some time. With growing fascination, I'm riveted on Kaye's end of the dialogue. When she hangs up, we stare at each other. Donna Bittner, after getting her MA from the California university last May, decided to go back home to Lincoln, Nebraska.

167

"For her summer vacation?"

No. Initially, Donna had applied to teach at McBee because it was in the Midwest, where she could be closer to her family. Then, after she got what had seemed like a promising phone interview, McBee had not contacted her again, not even to send an e-mail turning her down.

"Not contacted her? But you did!"

"I know, I know."

Donna hadn't wanted to seem pushy, according to the Coordinator, so she didn't call McBee to find out the status of the search, and in any case, she had begun to wonder if she wanted to work for a program that treated applicants so unprofessionally. Her father had been diagnosed with early onset Alzheimer's Disease. Her plan was that if she didn't get the McBee job, she would go back to Nebraska and live at home to be his full-time care-giver so that her mother could keep her teaching job. She packed up and went home to Lincoln, where she has been ever since. She sends the Coordinator and friends in the program postcards from there occasionally.

"But, Kaye, you offered her the job."

"Yes, I did. But—" Kaye sits back and gazes out the window for a few moments. Then she leafs through Donna's personnel file again and pulls out a copy of an e-mail. "Here it is."

After that first contact, Donna e-mailed Kaye to thank her for the interview and to say she would be staying with a friend for the summer and any official correspondence should be sent to the new address. Kaye was also asked to use a different phone number and a personal e-mail since Donna had finished her degree and no longer had a university e-mail.

"But her personal e-mail—"

"—must have been one she created using Donna's name in the address."

"In other words—"

"Our Donna Bittner isn't Donna Bittner."

"What?!" I'm flabbergasted. "How did she get the credentials? The transcript? The letters of recommendation?" Kaye shakes her head at the folder.

"It sounds like an inside job," I say, with Nancy Drew keenness. "Send them a picture of Donna and see if they recognize her."

Kaye brings up on her computer a digital photo of Donna from a Welcome to McBee ESL picnic in August. Kaye attaches it to an e-mail to California. In fifteen minutes the phone rings.

"Donna" had been a half-time temp secretary in the ESL Program that spring. Her name—at least the name she gave them—was Myrna Gratz. She was the one who transferred all the office calls. She also had access to official stationery, transcripts, resumés, recommendation letters, social security numbers, and who knows what else.

So there it is. Donna ... Myrna ... needs a better paying job than that of a minimum wage temp secretary and gets one without any qualifications except the ability to speak English and sing "The Rain in Spain" with a bad Cockney accent. Myrna Gratz? Somehow I find Donna's real name the most disconcerting aspect of the whole situation. I can't think of Donna Bittner as anyone but Donna Bittner.

"But Kaye, how could her paychecks here have been processed? Wouldn't the IRS and Social Security be on to her right away?"

"Well, she would have had access to Donna's social security number."

"That's a pretty big risk to take. The real Donna might have taken another job."

"According to the Coordinator, the real Donna's plans were formed in May and were quite firm."

"So fake Donna would have known that if real Donna got turned down by McBee, there would be no risk in taking her place. Real Donna wouldn't be drawing a paycheck."

Kaye shakes her head morosely.

"I didn't hear her voice again until she arrived here in August. I guess I should have been paying better attention, but I'm not sure I would have recognized a discrepancy after three months."

❖ ❖ ❖

Kaye will have to report it to the Dean as a possible case of identity theft.

"Just what we need right now, with the Dean's sights on our program," she says, staring at the memo on her desk. "We've been skating along on the strength of our good name. He'll be thrilled to hear we've let an unqualified instructor teach all semester."

She doesn't mean it as a thrust, I know. Her neck isn't flushed at all. She's too gloomy to be angry.

"I'm sorry it took so long for me to figure this out, Kaye. There were red flags fluttering all over the place. I was trying to give her the benefit of the doubt."

She sighs. "We all were. It's not your fault. But we can't fire her on the spot. Legal wheels will have to turn before we can accuse her." D. Renee Bittner's position at Worldwide Infotech Services will have to be verified. The California school will need to notify the real Donna and get law enforcement involved. It's a crime across state lines. Maybe the FBI will investigate.

"Leave this to me, now, Jane. Don't discuss it with Donna," Kaye says. "We've had this talk, but I don't need to remind you that University rules require strict confidentiality about personnel matters." Yet she is reminding me.

·32·

'M BACK IN my office when the phone rings.

I pick up, and before I say hello, a high-pitched voice I don't recognize greets me.

"Hi there, Jane."

"Hello. Who's calling, please?"

In a voice I do recognize the caller says, "It's Donna."

I take a breath. "Oh. Donna. You didn't sound like yourself."

"Didn't you look at your caller ID? I'm calling from down the hall. Or maybe you don't know about caller ID. That's okay. My grandma doesn't understand how it works either. I tell her, Gram, everybody has caller ID. You can identify calls from like a friend, or relative or even someone calling from a university." *Even someone calling from a university.* Subtle. "But there's nothing wrong with being old fashioned, Jane."

Caller ID. Why in the world hadn't I thought of that? Because I *am* old fashioned. I use a chalkboard, for God's sake. Worldwide InfoTech Services must have left the number for Donna to return my bogus call, and Donna could figure out right away who it was from. *Now* what? Do I just go ahead and admit to spying on her? But Kaye isn't ready to confront her, and I'm not supposed to discuss it with her. Anyway, maybe I have it wrong. Maybe she doesn't know what I've done. Oh boy.

"What ... uh ... what can I do for you, Donna?" I stammer.

"I had a question I wanted to run by you about an assignment. I'll be over in a sec."

"Actually, I have a student coming in—" But she's already hung up.

In a moment she walks in without a word, closes the door and sits down in Molly's swivel chair. She folds her arms across her chest and cocks her head to one side.

"I just wanted to find out if something was okay to allow. 'Cause I know you and Kaye are sticklers for following the rules, and I really want to be a team player."

Where is this going? I wait.

"One of my students wants to get credit for doing the same assignment in your class and my class, both."

This is not what I expect to hear.

"Well," I venture, "usually that's not allowed. What's the assignment?"

"I took your awesome advice and gave my students another project."

"Good."

"I'm having my students do some interviews—"

"Good idea."

"Thanks. So the students can choose who to interview and what to ask about. But Chika said—you know Chika Yamamoto?" I nod. "Chika said that in your class you already gave her the same homework."

"No, I haven't given an interview assignment—"

"Well, she says you assigned her to ask another student questions. Grammar questions. You said the other student's grades were dropping, and you thought it would help the student get more fired up to raise her grade. So, anyway, Chika wanted to know if she could also get credit in Communication Skills for that same assignment." Donna sits back in her chair and smiles blandly. "Can she?"

Now I do see where this is going.

"Well, uh …"

Donna shrugs out of her cardigan nonchalantly. "I mean it's all right with me. But I wasn't sure I could approve it anyway, because—not that I care—but wouldn't it violate that federal law—FEMA? FERMA? Whatever it's called? The one about student privacy you told me about?" She stops to look me straight in the eye. "The one that could get a teacher or a program sued if they violate it? Like telling one student that another student was getting low grades? Although …" She folds her sweater across her glittery bag. "… like, if no one finds out about it, who cares? We all have good reasons to bend rules sometimes. Don't we?" She purses her lips knowingly, activating those damn dimples. "You didn't think anything about taking those scarves at the time."

Scarves! She tucked that story away for future use. I flattered myself that I was comforting her with it. Yes indeed. It's made her quite comfortable.

I'm trying to process this information without showing the alarm that's ringing at a high decibel in my brain. *She's threatening me—and Kaye—into keeping her on.*

Donna sits back in Molly's chair. "If you catch my meaning?" she says calmly. We sit looking at each other.

Kaye knows nothing about my little scheme with Chika. She'll be furious. After all my promises to avoid this kind of ill-conceived, unethical meddling, I've made the program vulnerable to blackmail just when it's already precarious. I'll have to tell Kaye. If I thought Donna was taking liberties with her position before, imagine if she pulls me and the Program into her sordid spotlight. But regardless, Kaye can't keep her on. She'll simply have to let *both* of us go—Donna for fraud, me for misconduct. How will that go over with the Dean? He'll be delighted. Time to outsource! Kaye and everyone in the program will be on the street, all the students transferred into the clutches of *GET IN!*

There's a knock at the door. I jump in my seat. The door opens, and Chika pokes her head in.

"Oh, Chika," says Donna pleasantly, gesturing her in. "Just the girl we wanted to see."

Chika leans against the doorsill.

"Hi," she says disinterestedly.

"Go ahead and sit down," says Donna.

Chika sits.

"I was just talking to Jane about your interview assignment."

Chika protrudes her lips in a pout. "I forgot to put assignment on dropbox before midnight, but I finished. I should get credit. It's here." She starts rummaging through her backpack.

"I'm sorry, but Jane won't let you use her assignment for my class," says Donna, all sympathy.

Chika looks up. "I don't use it."

"You just said you finished it."

"I change my interview. I got new one, but not on computer yet. It's here. I can still get A? Even it's late?" She pulls two crumpled sheets of paper from her backpack. They're covered with her calligraphic scrawl running diagonally up the page, the questions embellished with doodles. "Yumi says I can't use grammar questions for two homeworks. She tell me to interview Bible study woman. I do it at cafeteria. I ask ten questions." She holds her paper up and reads from it. "'Who is Jesus?' (I already know, but I ask anyway), 'How he can die and still live?' 'Why you believe the impossible things like die and come back again—'?"

Donna scoots her chair closer to Chika's. "But when you were asking your grammar questions, you were trying to help Yumi, weren't you?" Here it comes. She's going to draw Chika into the extortion plan.

"I tried to increase grade."

"Well, you know, Jane shouldn't have discussed another students' grade with you. Grades are private. It's a very strict rule." Donna looks sidelong toward me. Her smile has returned.

Chika doesn't need to be reminded of the privacy rules. She learned them all too well after she unwillingly let us report her grades to her mother. And won't she enjoy getting me in trouble after my recalcitrance over her grade, to say nothing of my "fake" interest when she poured out her enthusiasm over *Ponyo*. What is the little Yumi scheme between us compared with the numerous gripes she has stored up over the semester? All those derisive snorts.

Chika darts a glance between Donna and me. She seems to think for a moment. Her eyes narrow. Then she turns back to Donna and opens those eyes wide with that expression of innocent bafflement I've come to know so well: her *What* homework? eyes.

"But it's okay Jane can discuss *my* grade. I give permission." What? What is she talking about?

Donna stands up quickly and the swivel chair rolls backward against Molly's desk.

"In this case, *Yumi* would have to give permission for Jane to discuss *her* grades with you."

"I don't know Yumi's grade," Chika says, folding her arms across her chest.

Donna now shakes her finger at Chika. "You told me Jane said Yumi's grade was decreasing, and you should ask her questions. To make her feel better."

Chika emits a dismissive puff of air and rolls her eyes. "Everybody know Yumi's grade is good. She's best in the class."

"That's not what—"

"*My* grade is decrease. Jane said ask to Yumi grammar questions. Yumi will help me. Like tutor."

"No," Donna's voice is becoming shrill, "you said that Jane told you *Yumi's* grade was decreasing. That's what you said."

Chika shrugs one shoulder. "My speaking is not so perfect. Maybe you don't understand my saying."

"You have an *A* in my Communication Skills class—"

"Yes, because I speak every day, but maybe sometimes I forget 'her' 'my' 'your,' like that. Use wrong word. You said it's okay speaking wrong. Just speaking every day in class is okay for increase fluently, don't worry about correct. You *said*!"

·33·

ON TUESDAY THE big news is the flight of Donna Bittner. Her flight is discovered when a student in Donna's 10:00 class calls Molly from the classroom to say that the students are there but Donna isn't. Molly checks Donna's cubicle.

Apparently she came back to her office the night before, took down her poster of the Mayan ruins at Tulum and the photo of herself holding up a margarita glass at a Cancún hotel bar, removed her yellow and black McBee Stingers stadium blanket that hung from the door peg, and took from her desk the Café Gulp plastic refill mug and the few knickknacks that have sat on her virtually empty bookshelves next to her three textbooks. The textbooks are no longer there.

Kaye has been informed. Had she already reported Donna's identity theft to the Dean? Or might that side of the affair go unmentioned? After all, a teacher's leaving two weeks before the end of the semester is regrettable, but not as deplorable as fraud. But what am I thinking? The investigation is probably already underway in California. It will inevitably end up at our door, and of course the real Donna needs to know what's going on.

Kaye's report to the Dean, it turns out, is still sitting on her desk waiting for a final proof read. She seems to be in unexpectedly good spirits.

"You're not worried?" I ask. "What does your report say?"

177

She raises an eyebrow at me. "Jane, you know it's confidential."

"But—"

"I'll only say that 'we are proud and grateful to have a teacher in our program astute enough to suspect identity theft and then go beyond the call of duty to prove it'." (She has just used air quotes.)

"Really? Not 'a teacher so stupid she didn't recognize an obvious identity thief until three months into the semester? Someone she was supposed to be mentoring closely'?"

"Glass-half-empty way of looking at it, Jane. The Dean claims he's a glass-half-full guy. He likes his faculty to shine before the public. 'Spin' is his middle name."

"And now it's yours."

"Well, I guess so," she says, smugly.

✳ ✳ ✳

To confirm the extent of Donna's iniquity, I go to the little ESL library and look upon the empty shelf where the pronunciation books are supposed to be kept. A string of black sequins linked by a broken thread lie on the tile under the book shelf. She's really gone. I sit down. Of course it's a relief. Yet, despite having been threatened and made a patsy of by this glittery con artist, I begin to feel inexplicably sorry for her. Images of Donna's child-like bling rise to mind. Her ingratiating earnestness, the eagerly poised pen, those slightly bulging eyes, the dimples. Donna must have had her reasons for the fraud—having to work a minimum wage temp job with no other prospects in this dreadful economy. Maybe a hidden chronic illness and no health insurance.

She must have held the common misconception that if you can speak English, surely you can teach it. She probably heard that ESL was where the jobs were, what with masses of well-to-do Chinese flocking to U.S. universities and internationals flooding the corporate service sector.

I picture Donna walking out the door last night in all her sparkling attire—still wearing open-toed rhinestone heels in winter—carrying her wholly inadequate office possessions. I feel guilty. I feel cruel. In spite of her trying to blackmail me, in spite of her depriving the real Donna of her livelihood, I wish I had been there when Donna—that is, Myrna—walked out the door, maybe to say, "Best of luck." At least she has the textbooks and pronunciation books. If she manages to evade the law, she can still pass herself off as an accent reduction expert in some other country, Mexico maybe, where she can drink tequila margaritas and trade lessons with her scuba instructor. Those dimples will take her far.

A little too much empathy, Jane. As always.

·34·

ON THE LAST DAY of the semester, Molly Askew-Ohashi and I are to meet our Low Intermediate students for a goodbye ceremony at Café Gulp in the back room away from the noise of the espresso machine. The students have written their final speeches in my class and rehearsed them individually with Molly.

I ask Chika to come in to the office before the speeches. Since Molly is working at her desk, I take Chika around the corner to Donna's—Myrna's—abandoned cubicle for privacy. We sit almost knee to knee in the small space. Chika jiggles her foot nervously, a habit probably triggered by being chastised in many offices over the course of her studies.

"Chika," I say quietly, "I want to thank you very much. You know that you brought back Yumi's happiness."

Chika arrests her foot mid-jiggle. She squints thoughtfully. "But maybe it's my fault made her depressed sometime," she says.

This from Chika surprises me. It was indeed Chika's fault—well, mine, too—but I wouldn't have given Chika credit for recognizing hers.

"Yumi got upset when I tell her she talk Japanese wrong. I think that gave her ashamed feeling."

What is she talking about? Some bit of spitefulness that I've missed?

"What do you mean? You told her she spoke Japanese wrong?"

"Yes," Chika admits. "Because she spoke Japanese with Korean way."

I stare at her. "You mean Yumi has a Korean accent?"

Chika shakes her head. "No accent, but ... one time, before we did fix-depression strategy, she scold me because I'm come late. She said, 'You come nine o'clock. Not after! *Ku-ji! Ku-ji!* Don't be rude to teacher.'"

"What's *ku-ji*?"

"It's mean nine o'clock in Japanese language. But she don't say like Japanese, *ku-ji*, with short sound. She say *ku-shi*, like Korean. I laughed at her and tease her. '*Ku-shi?*' Are you Korean?" And she look like nervous. She told me, 'I never say *shi*!' And I say, 'I know, but *this* time you *said*.' And then she don't talk to me."

It takes a moment before it sinks in. Then I feel the lurch in my heart. "But wasn't it just a mistake? A slip of the tongue? Because she was angry? Or she was tired? I remember she wasn't feeling well for a while. She might have been sick. Do you think it was just a mistake?"

"But it's strange sound. I think Japanese never make such mistake with *ji*, even they're tired."

Yumi's words all the way back in October, after the World War II fiasco echo in my mind: *Japan government must say sorry to Korean woman! Must give compensate money to them!* Yumi asserted it passionately to her Korean classmate, Mi-young, but in a confidential undertone. Say sorry to the comfort women.

I do the math in my head. Of course Yumi was too young to have been one of them herself; she would have been a baby at the end of the war. But some of those kidnapped "comfort" women had stayed in Japan, destitute and unable to pay their way home. Or in some cases their families in Korea had died during the war or were too ashamed to welcome them back. Most of the women had become sterile as a result of the continual rapes and infections from venereal disease, but a few of the women had given birth.

I have to be careful here. I don't want to put ideas in Chika's head if they're not already there. "I wonder why Yumi said '*ku-ji*' that way," I say casually.

Chika shrugs. "I don't know. Maybe she take class in Korean language sometime, like take English."

Yumi wouldn't have had a Korean accent if she had been raised in Japan from infancy, especially since those children and their mothers would have tried to hide their origins. But mightn't an elderly woman under stress inadvertently retrieve a bit of her mother's speech pattern? I imagine how those children and their mothers would have been treated in Japan. Denied citizenship and education, despised, shunned, ridiculed. Perhaps the mother had had no other way to support her child than to continue in the "service" of men. "*Your father was soldier!*" "*Your mother look so happy.*" "*I can't forgive my whole life.*"

How could I not have seen this? Yumi's despair—from a source deeper than mere guilt at violating the golden rule. That unthinkable past hovering close to the surface when she thought she had escaped it by being "saved," by being a "good Christian." That history rearing up and hurling her back into the old abyss of sorrow and shame simply because of a thoughtless homework assignment and her daily proximity to a privileged young Japanese girl who knew nothing of struggle and held her own good fortune—her respectable, concerned family—in contempt.

It seems Chika doesn't guess Yumi's secret, although surely she can tell the difference between Japanese and Korean faces—even *I* can usually see that difference after teaching students of the two nationalities for so long. But if Yumi is half Japanese, with Japanese perhaps dominant, and her face is old and … battered? How would

Chika or, for that matter, the Koreans and Chinese in the class guess? Or have they guessed? Maybe Mi-young has. She was the one to whom Yumi confided so quietly that "Japan government must say sorry to Korean woman."

Chika is only nineteen years old, ignorant of, and indifferent to, history. Of course she hasn't guessed. Right now she sits yawning in her chair. With no homework due on the last day, she's gone out barhopping with Allen the night before.

I should have guessed, though. If I had known the depths of Yumi's sorrow, mightn't I have done something differently? No, probably not. Yumi's tragedy was a secret closely held. What could I have done?

All things considered, maybe I did the best I could. And though I wonder how I've been so obtuse as to miss all the signs, still, I feel a little surge of pride that for Yumi's sake I at least put my neck out and defied the edicts of FERPA.

·35·

*A*T TWO P.M. most of the students have already arrived at the coffee house, pushed several tables together, and are ordering teas and café lattes.

As they remove their coats, they exclaim over each other's finery. Each has gotten dressed up for the going-away party. Mariam wears a traditional Indonesian *kebaya*—a fitted, flared lace brocade blouse over a long straight skirt, and a batik sash draped over her shoulder. An artificial purple orchid is pinned to her thick black hair. Heba is all in silk, from *hijab* to the hem of her long-sleeved, floor-length *dara'a* and her embroidered *thobe*. Several gold bracelets have been added to the usual collection on her wrists.

Jiho and Won wear gray suits and navy ties and look like mid-level Hyundai executives on their way up. Even Bing and Guill-ermo wear ties, Guillermo's over his sweat-shirt, Bing's over a Bart Simpson T-shirt. Guillermo's cap, in honor of the occasion, faces forward. Mi-young, who, even in class, dresses formally in low heels, straight skirts and fitted jackets that make her look like the well-paid administrative assistant of a Samsung CEO, today wears a rather low-cut blouse, the opening of which she unconsciously covers by pressing a hand to her chest.

Fiesta wears a pullover sweater embellished with a bright green, red, and white motif—snowflakes, sleigh with a Santa incongruously brandishing a vicious-looking whip over the backs of his reindeer.

Yumi apparently pin curled her perm-damaged hair the night before, because it's brushed out in sumptuous curls, which she keeps patting as if to be sure she hasn't dreamed them. Otherwise, she wears her Iowa Sunday church outfit—an over blouse with knee-length skirt, stockings and white leather New Balance walking shoes. I study her closely. She looks happy. She looks restored.

Chika's mini-skirt is even shorter than usual, and the effect enhances the precariousness of her black fishnet stockings, held up on her long legs by loose elastic at mid-thigh. She is shod in '50s tennis shoes with orange laces that nicely match the re-touched orange of her bangs.

I myself am dolled up in the red velvet dress I bought for my niece's wedding. Molly comes in from the cold, shedding her earbuds and Nepalese woolen caftan and shaking snow out of the thick nimbus of curls that serve her as warmly as a stocking cap.

But it is Masoud who steals the show. There are gasps and an abrupt setting down of mugs when he walks through the door and takes off his coat. Everyone is so used to seeing him, small and thin and apologetic, rushing into class in his green Sanicorp uniform, always out of breath from his effort to be on time. Today he commands the room, seeming tall and benevolent in the full traditional dress of Zanzibar: a long white robe and white embroidered cap. Even Chika seems a little star struck by him.

"King Masoud!" cries Guillermo.

The cameras come out en masse, and for fifteen minutes a frenzy of picture taking follows. Everyone has to be photographed next to the noble Masoud and gorgeous Heba and Mariam. Then they need group shots with Molly and me, shots of Molly and me by ourselves, single shots of everyone. Eventually, the Café Gulp espresso server is enlisted to work her way through the pile of cameras set on the table, and patiently, to cries of "cheese!" "chiizu" (Japanese), "whiskey" (Latin American), "kimchi" (Korean), "qiězi" ("eggplant" in

Chinese) etc., takes shot after shot of the whole group until at last all are satisfied and the students can't put off their speeches any longer.

* * *

We take our seats and there is that nervous quiet in which each student tries not to look like someone who would want to go first.

Finally, Mariam volunteers. Molly has worked with her on this speech for a week to get the kinks out of her idiosyncratic grammar, but in the fervor of performance, she reverts back to her barely comprehensible, stream-of-consciousness syntax, ending with a promise to bring her brother Agus from Indonesia to McBee next semester because he is "very impressing my English to be better than I came here for three months ago."

Heba rises next in all her silken elegance and talks about being one step closer to her goal of becoming an eye surgeon, thanks be to Allah and the excellent English teachers at McBee. She hands Molly and me two enormous shrink-wrapped slabs of rather congealed-looking dates from Kuwait. It's okay; they aren't silk scarves and can be shared with everyone. We accept the gift with effusive expressions of gratitude.

Mariam and Heba push Fiesta to her feet, knowing that otherwise she will wait in misery until the very last, too traumatized by then to speak at all. Fiesta clings to her notes, fastens her eyes on Molly's face and takes a long stertorous breath before speaking. She and Molly have spent several sessions in the privacy of our office breathing together and practicing voice projection, but now Fiesta looks gray around the gills, and I find myself deep breathing on her behalf to vicariously prevent a possible fainting spell. But then Fiesta finds her voice and the result is very sweet.

"This semester I have two good friends encourage me do my best. They are beautiful, kind ladies, Mariam and Heba." Mariam's eyes glitter. She puts her arm through Heba's, and the two lean into each other like parents at a child's graduation. "I think I speak more now than before. But still not enough. So because good friends, good classmates, good teachers, next semester I will push my English hardly and never afraid to speak. Thank you." Heba and Mariam ease her down between them amidst the cheers and applause, and Heba blots Fiesta's damp forehead with the tail end of her jade green silk scarf.

Next comes Masoud, standing straight, with his arms at his sides. In his white garb he seems a man in charge of his destiny. After thanks to Allah, me, Molly, and each and every person at the table, he says he is looking forward to the three-week winter break. "I will play with my Ali, I will sleep, sleep, and sleep more. But—" He pauses for effect. "—I will *dream* in English!"

Jiho rises to Guillermo's call for "Question Man!"

"I always ask to teachers 'Why?' 'Why?' 'Why?'" says Jiho. "But my teachers are always patient to my questions—" Just then Jiho's cell phone rings. He opens it and quickly glances at the caller ID. Apologizing, he ducks his head and puts the phone to his ear. "What? … When? … Where?" he says into it, and looks around, puzzled at his classmates' explosion of laughter.

Mi-young speaks of her initial culture shock, her many misunderstandings with her U.S. roommate, and how "I was so relief I can come to my class and even cry there. And Chika—" Startled, Chika glances up from tugging on her stockings. "—always gave good explaining because she knows many knowledges of English idiom. Everybody helped me. Thank you very much everybody." She sits down, flushed.

As Bing talks, he smooths the tip of the long, unfamiliar necktie over his round belly. His apple cheeks look plumper than ever. "I want to say to our teachers I'm sorry I was not so good student this semester. But you don't feel bad because I will give you most exciting time of your life. *Exciting*," he emphasizes. "The *most* exciting!" I raise an eyebrow at Molly. The proposal sounds almost risqué. But he's just demonstrating his mastery of the superlative. "Just you have to write in the gradebooks A, A, A, A, A, A and next semester I give you—I *will* give you—a ride in the best car in the world, the Bugatti Veyron 16.4 coupe." I glance happily at Molly. All his superlatives *and* articles right! Yes! "This is not bribe," he continues. "Only suggestion. Thank you." Well, maybe not the articles.

Guillermo has something gently teasing to say about each of his classmates, calling them by the various nicknames he has bestowed on them and professing to miss them next semester when he will have to repeat Low Intermediate while they will be soaring up to Intermediate or even High Intermediate levels. This is just modesty. He has ended up with a solid B average. In honoring Yumi, he reiterates his various nicknames for her (Paparazzi Yumi, Actress Yumi, Sushi Chef Yumi, Dr. Yumi), any one of which suits her, but Grammar Grandma is his most fitting one. Everyone, even I, younger by only two years, claim her as our Grammar Grandma. Finally Guillermo thanks his teachers for not smacking his fingers with a ruler, in the manner of his grade school teachers in El Salvador, who employed this punishment daily to cure him (unsuccessfully) of clowning.

Like Guillermo, Chika, too has in the last three weeks of the semester miraculously pulled out a C+ average, which allows her to move up to Intermediate level at last, trumping her grandmother's objections to her wasting time in "go nowhere." Perhaps this success explains her uncharacteristic charitableness; she thanks us and her classmates for our help and apologizes for "sometimes not pay attention very much and have bad mood." She turns and speaks directly to Yumi, who, having settled in a rather low armchair, appears only as an extravagantly permed head at the end of the table. My jaw clenches.

"If I could be old and have good mind as Yumi, so I would be happy," Chika vows. "So I think I must start now." I let my jaw relax.

Yumi's chin is trembling.

Silent Won stands up then, perhaps to take the attention off Yumi and give her a chance to compose herself. Before starting, he stands quietly as if—having waited a long time to say something worth breaking his public silence for—he wants everyone to appreciate the gravity of the moment. He thanks his classmates individually, detailing specific ways in which his life has been enriched by having known them. His audience is rather awed by this unexpected performance, and those at the extreme ends of the table press forward and cup their ears to hear.

"And also," he says, "I like to give thank you to Yumi, my best classmate. She is so good woman to help us. She has pure heart and good spirit, like grandmother—"

"Grammar Grandma!" breaks in Guillermo, inciting spontaneous cheers.

Won waits soberly for the cheering to subside.

"If we Koreans do not know Yumi," he resumes, "we would not accept to learn English is fun and enjoyment. And we would not know how good and kind can be the older Japanese. I want to meet her again in future." Bowing low to her, he says, "Thank you, Yumi, our grandmother." I glance at Yumi's face to detect anything in her expression that betrays a knowledge of the inadvertent irony of Won's declaration. She seems bemused by his praise. Korean war wounds are still fresh after sixty-four years, even among young Koreans like Won. Yet even believing her to be Japanese, he still gives her the honorific title Grandmother. Yumi puts her hand to her cheek and then to her lips, covering her mouth. It's only when I see the crinkling at the corners of her eyes that I realize Yumi is controlling the urge to laugh. What could she be laughing about but the irony?

It's a relief when Won turns his attention away from Yumi to Molly and me, even though I imagine I've disappointed him a little by not quite meeting the strict standards imposed by his English teachers in Korea.

"Finally," he says, "thanks to our teachers. They teach to speak English correctly is not just only the rules but is like a dancing. I must be free a little so I can discover the natural way. So I very thank you, our teachers."

Now there's only Yumi left, and Guillermo, pounding on the table with his teaspoon, starts the chant: "Yu-mi! Yu-mi! Yu-mi!"

Yumi wipes her eyes under her glasses with a napkin and slowly stands up. I hug myself, my heart beating a little faster. With a flurry of bows and thank you's, Yumi begins.

"When I was child—when I was *a* child—I everyday wished I could go away to somewhere. I thought if I am perfect girl, maybe I can fly away." She looks down into her tea cup. "I was ugly girl, wrong-talking, not belonging, jealous girl. And I could not fly away. I could never fly away." She raises her eyes and looks around at all the attentive faces. Returned now is her old glad smile, deepening the wrinkles in her cheeks. "Now I'm old woman and I fly to here. Not with wish-wings but by airplane. I think better it's late than never. Here is the best time in my life because kind teachers and friends. Next semester I stay in McBee. And when I finish English study, I will study Bible more and maybe, if God wish, I might become pasta. Or ..." She looks above the heads of her audience as if the thought has just occurred to her, "Or I study English more and maybe ... I become teacher. I will come back Japan and teach English ..." she nods archly in the direction of Guillermo, "to naughty boys."

Guillermo stands up. "I will come to Japan, be your student. Pay you anything."

She nods at Guillermo, but is she really thinking of Chika? Forgiving this naughty girl for the privileged girlhood of which she herself was robbed?

"This is the best time of my life," Yumi says again. "Everybody helped me too much. Thank you, thank you." She sinks down into her low chair and looks up from it humbly like a little sand crab who has just scuttled halfway into its hole to observe the world from a place of security.

The applause for Yumi's speech, accompanied by Guillermo's earsplitting whistle, is so loud and long, the espresso machine worker leans around the doorway curiously.

Molly's and my speeches, although required for a ceremonious end to the proceedings, are anti-climactic and redundant in our praise for the students' hard work and exceptional camaraderie.

❆ ❆ ❆

After the speeches, the students begin to meander away in two's and three's except for Won, Jiho, and Heba, who walk purposefully off to the library to take one last shot at cramming for the next morning's TOEFL exam. At Low Intermediate level, they don't stand a chance of passing, but they cherish the superstitious hope that all their shot-in-the-dark guesses will be lucky ones.

Allen comes to whisk Chika away. Molly hurries off to finish her grading.

Yumi stands by the door with Mi-young, deep in a discussion of airport shuttle and flight schedules. As I approach, Yumi beams up at me. "Mi-young invite me to winter break in Korea with Mi-young's family. She is so kind to invite me. I never see Korea. Now because bad economy, almost airlines give away cheap ticket." As she speaks, Yumi is giving her young friend's arm tender little pats.

"That's wonderful!" It takes me a moment to grasp the significance of this news. Hadn't Yumi already accepted her "pasta's" and her Bible teacher's offers of refuge over the holidays? Instead, Yumi is going to Korea. Going home? I will never know for sure.

·36·

*O*N FRIDAY I HAND IN my final grade reports and return my textbooks to their shelves when Doug Best e-mails from the airport en route from Brazil to say that Rosa's father has died and the funeral is over. They will be back late that night and will come by my house on Saturday morning to pick up the clumbers if that's okay.

I lean back heavily in my chair.

If that's okay.

Is it okay that tonight will be the last time Sheryl and Sue will greet me at the top of the basement stairs, wagging their plumy tails? Okay that I will have to rely on classical radio from now on instead of squeaking Mr. Bill to get me up in the morning? I'm not sure it is okay. Perhaps it's not okay.

But there's nothing to be done about it. It was all very well for friends to say, Jane, you need a dog. I hadn't wanted a dog. But I don't want *not* to have these particular dogs that I do have. It's confusing to be a non-dog person and then find yourself suddenly reluctant to relinquish two dogs that have been foisted on you temporarily.

When I get home, I let Sheryl and Sue out into the backyard and stand by the door watching them race maniacally around the yard after each other, rolling and leaping, standing off, bottoms in the air and forefeet apart, daring the other to make the first move, then up and running again. I pick up a tennis ball and take the Chuck-It from the key hook by the door. This will be my last fling, so to speak, and I decide to do it until I, or they, are too worn out to go on. A half hour later, we're all three panting, grinning, and still good to go. I've shrugged off my coat by this time and switched the ball flinger to my left hand.

At 6:30 I bring them inside. After dinner I make a fire and sit before it, reading *The Dollmaker*, a novel so perfect I'm reading it for the fourth time, but so heartbreaking I know I will once again stop reading before the climax of the story. Sue is investigating a beetle in the wood box, and Sheryl stands leaning against my easy chair like a sleepy sentinel. Well, everything comes to an end—crises, semesters, dog care. Enjoy the sweet moments while you can.

I put the clumbers out one last time before going to bed, and after tidying the kitchen and packing up the bulk of the squeak toys and other paraphernalia on the chance that Doug and Rosa come early, I open the back door to bring the dogs in. Tongues lolling cheerfully, Sheryl and Sue stand on the patio with a dead rabbit at their feet.

I let out an involuntary cry and drop to my knees. I put out a hand to touch the rabbit's fur, thick and soft and so deep I can bury my fingers in it. Underneath the fur the flesh has already grown cold.

There is no blood. One of the dogs has broken its neck with a sharp jerk, probably after the other dog drove the rabbit into its jaws.

The clumbers watch patiently as I kneel before the rabbit—my rabbit—my mysterious frolicker in snow, my disdainer of morning glory blossoms, despoiler of pansies, portrait poser, this rabbit I once wished killed by the beagle with the rusty voice. Toward the clumbers I feel no anger; I feel only a heaviness on my heart. The corpse is so unalterably still, all its keen alertness and agility, its quivering sensitivity drained out of it.

I don't know what to do with the body. The ground is too frozen for me to dig a hole. After some thought, I decide just to leave it there for the night. Some other creature might carry it off, and if not, I'll call the city in the morning and have Animal Control take it away.

I pull Sheryl and Sue inside by their collars, but it isn't necessary; they seem quite disinterested in the rabbit now that they have killed it. They've done their job—all in a day's work. In the basement, they sniff routinely at their empty food bowls as if it doesn't occur to them that they could have had rabbit for a bedtime snack.

I dream about the rabbit that night. I dream it's alive again, standing on its hind legs chewing on a squeak toy to prove it isn't dead. In the morning I take the clumbers out the front way for a quick walk and keep them in the kitchen while I venture onto the back patio.

The stiff, still corpse is exactly as I left it. Rays of morning sun reflect in its dead open eye and shed a pink light on its white and brown markings. In that clear morning sunlight, I see at once that this rabbit isn't *the* rabbit but *a* rabbit. Not my definite specific already known rabbit. An *in*definite *non*specific one that I don't know, whose whiskers are short and gray instead of long and black, whose white front paws lack the telltale rust-colored stain I drew so carefully in pastels.

"Thank you!" I say aloud. "Thank you for being the wrong rabbit." And I'm glad no one I know is around to hear the elation in my voice since this animal, too, is a sentient being, who has been killed, yet I don't feel sad for it in the same way I would for the other. And *that*, I remember, as if I have not learned it so many, many times before, is what one has to try to change in oneself. To try to think of everyone as *the* and not *a*. To help those who have only half an idea, if any, about a person from Kuwait or Zanzibar or Korea to shift their thinking from the unknown to the particular. I feel grateful to be making a living at a job that turns indefinite peoples into definite ones. Not a spoiled brat, but the young girl whose dreams are being frustrated. Not a fawning imposter, but the woman who loves sparkle and is proud of her bosom and needs, for whatever reason, to become someone she is not. The definite article. "It's the only way we will ever get along in this world," I tell the clumbers, as I dial Animal Control to pick up the rabbit—the innocent, unlucky rabbit who tried, valiantly, to outrace the clever clumber spaniels, who like to make things squeak and were bred to hunt.

KATE KASTEN is the author of three other novels: *Better Days*, *The Deconversion of Kit Lamb*, and *Ten Small Beds*, as well as a book of fairy tales for adults, *Wildwood: Fairy Tales and Fables Re-imagined*. Her short fiction has been published in *Glimmer Train*, *American Literary Review*, and *Northwest Review*. She has also co-authored, with Sandra de Helen, *The Clue in the Old Birdbath*, a musical satire of the Nancy Drew mystery genre. Her humorous monologues can be found on her YouTube channel, *boomeronachair*. Kasten lives and writes in Iowa City, Iowa, where she is retired from twenty-five years of teaching English as a Second Language.

Made in the USA
Lexington, KY
29 April 2017